U0031663

——著

畢業後移居倫敦，進入時尚界和社交圈。他曾從事各種文學活動，出版詩集、小說《格雷的畫像》、《快樂王子與其他故事》等，並以喜劇《溫夫人的扇子》、《不可兒戲》成為維多利亞時代晚期倫敦最著稱的劇作家之一。

正當王爾德的名聲成功達到頂峰，他被判處「嚴重猥褻罪」，兩年後獲釋，之後前往法國，並在當地去世。

 顏湘如————————— 譯

自由譯者，譯著包括《終結狩獵的女孩》、《畫鳥的人》、《消失的另一半》、《手斧男孩．落難童年求生記》、《別相信任何人》、《S.》、《人生複本》、《龍紋身女孩》系列等。

快 樂 王 子
The Happy Prince

奧斯卡·王爾德 ———— 著 顏湘如 ———— 譯

野人

轟轟烈烈的人生才能雋永不朽：
《快樂王子》文學特輯

十九世紀末，英美颳起一陣「王爾德」風潮，這陣旋風的中心人物正是愛爾蘭作家奧斯卡‧王爾德（一八五四一一九〇〇）。他創造了一波波備受眾人推崇的潮流，是當時社交界和時尚圈的未來之星。王爾德擁有超凡的個人魅力和浪漫唯美的個性，標誌性的奇裝異服永遠多彩繽紛。除此之外，王爾德幽默、犀利，講起話來口若懸河，人們被他機智的巧言妙語以及豐富的文學創作所深深吸引，他因此變得聲名大噪。但隨著名氣增長，爭議如影隨形，緊緊地纏縛著王爾德。

一八九五年，心高氣傲的風流人物終於被拽下神壇，落得身敗名裂的下場。王爾德被情人父親控告猥褻罪，必須面臨法律審判。無奈他依然贏不了社會輿論與封閉的法律，最終仍免不了牢獄之災。

在保守的年代，王爾德選擇將人生活得轟轟烈烈，迎接所有的大起大落；但到了二十一世紀的現代，王爾德除了是英國文學史上的標誌性人物，更是酷兒文化中被奉為偶像的存在。正是如此神采飛揚的他，才會雋永不朽地活在歷史中，見證自己如何改變了全世界。

🍁 我們都困在陰溝，但仍有人選擇仰望星空
　　——王爾德的文學旅程

　　王爾德是十九世紀末英國的著名作家，他的作品詞藻華麗、主題新鮮、觀點明確、文類多元，也十分膾炙人口。許多佳句流傳至今，成為許多人心目中的至理名言。他的戲劇作品享譽維多利亞時代晚期的各大戲院，讓他成為當時倫敦最著名的劇作家之一。此外，他的散文、小說、短篇故事、評論、論文等依然在文學史上熠熠生輝，一八八八年出版的童話集《快樂王子與其他故

王爾德。由美國攝影師拿破崙‧薩洛尼（Napoleon Sarony）拍攝於一八八二年。

事》是他寫給兩個兒子的故事，日後這部作品成為了全球讀者一生必讀的溫馨作品。

　　一八九二年，王爾德出版他的第一部諷世喜劇《溫夫人的扇子》（*Lady Windermere's Fan*）。乍看之下，這部作品機智又詼諧，但其實藏著貴族婦女被迫妥協、放下堅持的無奈。這部作品也誕生了如今依然廣為流傳的名言：

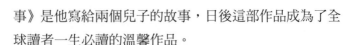

　　「我們都困在陰溝裡，但仍有人選擇仰望星空。」
　　"We are all in the gutter but some of us are looking at the stars"

　　《溫夫人的扇子》大獲成功，讓王爾德在當時一炮而紅，成為劇作界炙手可熱的明星。然而，說到王爾德的經典戲劇，大家肯定會想到他的喜劇代表作《不可兒戲》（*The Importance of Being Earnest*），這部作品也是他一八九五年創作的最後一部戲劇。這齣通俗喜劇顯得荒謬，看似沒有什麼偉大的創作動機，但幽默又充滿諷刺的劇情反映了當時上流社交圈的趨炎附勢，以及貴族之間僵硬的裝腔作態，讓人性的虛偽和惡劣無所遁形。

　　王爾德的戲劇作品在他生前獲得極大迴響，並帶來錢財與名聲；但他創作的短篇小說在當時雖充滿了爭議，後世的文學界卻是青睞有加。一八九〇年，王爾德先在雜誌上刊登了《格雷的畫像》（*The Picture of Dorian*

THIS NUMBER CONTAINS

The Picture of Dorian Gray.

By OSCAR WILDE.

COMPLETE.

JULY, 1890

LIPPINCOTT'S

MONTHLY MAGAZINE

CONTENTS

PRICE TWENTY-FIVE CENTS

J: B: LIPPINCOTT: Co: PHILADELPHIA:

LONDON: WARD, LOCK & CO.

PARIS: BRENTANO'S, 17 AVENUE DE L'OPÉRA.

一八九〇年七月，〈格雷的畫像〉於*Lippincot's*月刊雜誌上首次出版。

Gray），隔年才出版成書。當時，這部作品在英國掀起了爭議，不少媒體和群眾紛紛批評此篇作品「不道德」、「粗俗」，甚至在一八九五年針對他的審判中，因為小說劇情涉及男性間的愛情而被原告上交法庭，成為證實王爾德「同性戀」罪刑的證物。

王爾德的文學作品和他本人的時尚打扮一樣，一掃維多利亞時期常見的拘謹和實用主義，以美麗、浪漫的文字，追求著華麗以及純然的藝術之美。因為獨一無二的風格，他被推崇為唯美主義的先鋒，以及劃時代的文學界偶像。

✿ 藝術不必有意義，但一定要美得華麗
　　——王爾德與唯美主義

在維多利亞時代晚期，大約從十九世紀後半開始，工業革命帶來的唯物主義和進步主義逐漸式微。在頹廢主義的催化下，英國藝術與文學界開始推崇所謂的「唯美主義」（Aestheticism）。從前，人們認為藝術創作具有傳授道德、說教等目的，必須言之有物；但對於唯美主義的提倡者而言，藝術是至高無上的存在，它不需要具備任何實質上的意義。唯美主義藝術家一心只為創造出感官上的享受，他們追求頹廢、華麗、矛盾所營造的美

感，並相信純粹的「美」才至臻完美，才是藝術存在的真正意義。

唯美主義的浪潮中，奧斯卡‧王爾德是唯美主義精神的代表性人物。在牛津大學就讀期間，王爾德認識了兩位導師：提出「為藝術而藝術」的華特‧佩特（Walter Pater），以及英國文學界與藝術界的知名學者兼評論家約翰‧羅斯金（John Ruskin）。在兩位導師的薰陶與支持下，王爾德認為藝術至高無上。在《格雷的畫像》序言中，王爾德明白地寫下：「在美麗事物中尋找醜陋涵義的人皆是迂腐、毫無魅力的，他們犯下了大錯。」這世上沒有「所謂道德之書與不道德之書。書籍只有寫得好和寫得不好，就這樣而已」。文末，他下了定論：「所有藝術都挺沒用的。」

王爾德真切地活出了唯美主義的精神，像他這麼浪漫的男人，一生雖然顛簸，但肯定充滿傳奇性。講到這裡，不得不提到王爾德的代表性事件——違反「性悖軌法」的審判。一八八五年，英國通過「拉布謝爾修正案」（Labouchere Amendment），刑期明訂為兩年苦役。十年後，王爾德遭同性愛人阿爾弗雷德‧道格拉斯勳爵（Lord Alfred Douglas）的父親昆斯伯里侯爵（Marquess of Queensberry）公開指責違反上述法案，王爾德因而以誹謗罪起訴侯爵。敗訴後，王爾德反被侯爵公開控告「嚴重猥褻」與「雞姦」，雙方自此展開訴訟。法庭上，王爾

諷刺唯美主義的畫作《皇家學院的私人景觀（A Private View at the Royal Academy）》。王爾德位於畫面中間偏右，被一群女人和小孩簇擁著。由畫家威廉·鮑爾·弗里思（William Powell Frith）繪於一八八一年。

德慷慨陳述著「不敢說出名字的愛」：

> 「⋯⋯這愛在本世紀被誤解了，以至於它可能被描
> 述成『不敢說出名字的愛』，並且由於這個誤解，
> 我現在站在了這裡。這愛是美麗的，是精緻的，是
> 最高貴的愛的形式，它沒有一絲一毫不自然，它是
> 智慧的，並循環地存在於年長男性與年輕男性之間，
> 只要年長者有智慧，而年輕者看到了他生命中全部
> 的快樂、希望以及魅力。以至於這愛本該如此，而
> 這個世界卻不能理解，這個世界嘲笑它，有時竟然
> 讓這愛中之人成為眾人的笑柄。」

雖然王爾德極力為自己辯護，他依然被定罪、入獄
服刑兩年。出獄後，在據說曾經交往過的故友羅伯特・
羅斯（Robert Ross）的幫助下，王爾德移居巴黎，並在那
裡度過餘生。

王爾德除了是唯美主義的代言人，他被捕入獄的悲
劇更是唯美主義時期的代表性事件。在能夠逃罪、苟活
的情況下，為了證明心中堅信的愛，王爾德選擇讓鐐銬
扣在自己身上，成為接受世人歧視、審判與罵聲的殉道
者。然而，王爾德也因此成為同性戀運動的文化偶像。
在王爾德出獄後八十年，英國於一九六七年將男性之間
的性行為除罪化。世界正在變得寬容，變得願意接受那

紐約Straiton & Storm's雪茄
廣告使用了王爾德的肖像畫
做為宣傳，文案中強調「唯
美」。

曾經「不敢說出名字的愛」。

　　王爾德死後葬在巴黎拉雪茲神父公墓（Cimetiere du
Pere Lachaise），他的墓碑參考了自己詩集《斯芬克斯》
（Sphinx）中獅身人面天使的形象，現已成為法國的國家
文物。王爾德的墓碑吸引全球人民前來景仰，許多女性
造訪時會在雕像上留下自己的紅唇印以致上愛慕之意，

王爾德與阿爾弗雷德·道格拉斯勳爵（攝於一八九三年）。

羅伯特·羅斯，王爾德的摯友，謠傳為王爾德第一個同性情人。

只是人們獻上的親吻多到差點腐蝕了雕像，王爾德的後裔不得不裝上透明隔板來保護墓碑。

　　而在王爾德的家鄉——愛爾蘭都柏林，他的紀念雕像就設立在故居對面的廣場。雕像不拘小節地斜倚在石頭上，他手持菸斗、穿著鮮綠色和豔紅色的上衣，神情囂張得不可一世，正如本尊一般肆意灑脫，這不禁讓人聯想到他筆下的快樂王子，只是雖然同樣眼中映著眾生百態，王爾德卻選擇笑對荒謬人生。

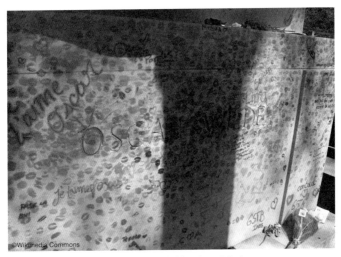

王爾德墓碑上布滿朝聖者的唇印（攝於二〇一〇年）。

王爾德在都柏林的雕像（攝於二〇〇七年）。

✿ 絕望中承載希望的成人美學童話
——《快樂王子與其他故事》

〈快樂王子〉是王爾德最受歡迎的短篇故事,既有童話色彩,又獲得了普世愛戴。故事從快樂王子的視角,諷刺了富有階級對現實狀況的漠視,以及對底層人民的關懷。多情的燕子甘願留在寒冬,為快樂王子實踐善行;快樂王子雖然沒有行動能力,卻心甘情願地為了需要的人褪去身上的寶石和金箔。漸漸地,快樂王子不再是耀眼的雕像,也不再被視為藝術品,但他卻為社會上許多可憐人帶來實質的幫助與改善。

在短短故事中,我們看到了許多華麗又鮮活的場面,例如漂亮的快樂王子雕像、燕子與王子溫馨的感情,以及角色最真實、最貼近人性的反應。除此之外,故事中也反映了純真、善良、純粹的愛、同理心、分享……等美德,讓讀者不禁深深自我反思。

王爾德是唯美主義的擁護者,時時強調著藝術的純粹之美。快樂王子褪下了外在的美麗,才能為社會帶來用處;同樣地,〈快樂王子〉不只美麗,故事內容也值得深思。自二十世紀中開始,這部傑出的作品陸續被改編成廣播劇、電影、音樂、動畫等形式,讓更多人被〈快樂王子〉的魅力以及王爾德的天才所驚豔。

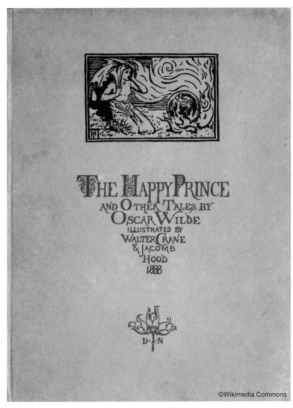

快樂王子一八八八年初版書封，由英國畫家喬治・珀西・傑康一胡德（George Percy Jacomb-Hood）繪製。

快樂王子

———————— ❧ ————————

— ❧ The Happy Prince ❧ —

城市上空，一根高高的圓柱上，矗立著快樂王子的雕像。他全身綴滿薄薄的純金箔，兩隻眼睛是晶亮的藍寶石，劍柄上還有一顆大紅寶石熠熠生輝。

快樂王子備受大家讚譽。「他就像風信雞那樣美麗。」某位市議員說道，他希望博得具有藝術眼光的美名，隨後卻又補上一句：「只是沒那麼實用。」唯恐民眾以為他不切實際，他其實不是那樣的人。

「你怎麼就不能學學快樂王子？」一位通情達理的母親對哭著討月亮的小兒子說：「快樂王子再怎麼樣也不會哭哭鬧鬧。」

「真慶幸這世上還有人這麼快樂。」一名失意男子凝視著這尊令人讚嘆的雕像，喃喃自語。

「他看起來就像天使一樣。」走出大教堂的育幼院童說道，他們身穿亮麗的深紅斗篷和潔白的圍兜裙。

「你們怎麼知道？你們又沒看過天使。」數學老師說。

「有啊，我們在夢裡看過。」院童們說，數學老師聽了皺起眉頭，一臉嚴肅，因為他不贊成孩子們做夢。

某天晚上，有一隻小燕子飛越城市上空。他的朋友在六星期以前就飛往埃及，但他留下來，因為他愛上了最美的蘆葦。早春時分，他尾隨一隻黃色大飛蛾沿河而下，邂逅了蘆葦，深受她的纖纖細腰所吸引，便停下來與她攀談。

H igh above the city, on a tall column, stood the statue of the Happy Prince. He was gilded all over with thin leaves of fine gold, for eyes he had two bright sapphires, and a large red ruby glowed on his sword-hilt.

He was very much admired indeed. "He is as beautiful as a weathercock," remarked one of the Town Councillors who wished to gain a reputation for having artistic tastes; "only not quite so useful," he added, fearing lest people should think him unpractical, which he really was not.

"Why can't you be like the Happy Prince?" asked a sensible mother of her little boy who was crying for the moon. "The Happy Prince never dreams of crying for anything."

"I am glad there is some one in the world who is quite happy," muttered a disappointed man as he gazed at the wonderful statue.

"He looks just like an angel," said the Charity Children as they came out of the cathedral in their bright scarlet cloaks and their clean white pinafores.

"How do you know?" said the Mathematical Master, "you have never seen one."

"Ah! but we have, in our dreams," answered the children; and the Mathematical Master frowned and looked very severe, for he did not approve of children dreaming.

One night there flew over the city a little Swallow. His friends had gone away to Egypt six weeks before, but he had stayed behind, for he was in love with the most beautiful Reed. He had met her early in the spring as he was flying down the river after a big yellow moth,

「我可以愛你嗎？」燕子說，他喜歡單刀直入，蘆葦只是對他深深彎腰。燕子繞著她飛啊飛，偶爾以翅膀點水，河面泛起銀色漣漪。這是他追求的方式，持續了整個夏天。

「這樣的迷戀太可笑了。」其他燕子嘰嘰啾啾地說：「她又沒錢，還那麼一大堆親戚。」說得也是，河邊的確長滿蘆葦。而當秋天來臨，燕子全都飛走了。

同伴走後，燕子開始覺得孤單，也開始厭倦了曾經心儀的蘆葦。「她都不說話，」他說道：「而且我擔心她太愛賣弄風騷，因為她老是和風調情。」沒錯，每當風一吹，蘆葦便會以最優美的身姿行屈膝禮。他接著又說：「我承認她宜室宜家，但我喜愛旅行，我的妻子自然也應該喜愛旅行。」

「你願意跟我走嗎？」燕子終於問了蘆葦，但蘆葦搖頭，她太戀家了。「原來你一直在玩弄我，」他高喊道：「我要出發去金字塔了，再見！」說完便逕自飛走。

他飛了一整天，入夜後來到這座城市。「要上哪過夜呢？」他自問：「但願這座城已經為我做好準備。」

這時他看見高聳柱子上的雕像。

「就在那裡過夜。」他大喊：「那位置好，空氣很清新。」於是他飛落快樂王子的雙腳之間。

「我有個金色臥室呢。」他四下環視輕輕自語，然後

and had been so attracted by her slender waist that he had stopped to talk to her.

"Shall I love you?" said the Swallow, who liked to come to the point at once, and the Reed made him a low bow. So he flew round and round her, touching the water with his wings, and making silver ripples. This was his courtship, and it lasted all through the summer.

"It is a ridiculous attachment," twittered the other Swallows; "she has no money, and far too many relations"; and indeed the river was quite full of Reeds. Then, when the autumn came they all flew away.

After they had gone he felt lonely, and began to tire of his lady-love. "She has no conversation," he said, "and I am afraid that she is a coquette, for she is always flirting with the wind." And certainly, whenever the wind blew, the Reed made the most graceful curtseys. "I admit that she is domestic," he continued, "but I love travelling, and my wife, consequently, should love travelling also."

"Will you come away with me?" he said finally to her; but the Reed shook her head, she was so attached to her home.

"You have been trifling with me," he cried. "I am off to the Pyramids. Good-bye!" and he flew away.

All day long he flew, and at night-time he arrived at the city. "Where shall I put up?" he said; "I hope the town has made preparations."

Then he saw the statue on the tall column.

"I will put up there," he cried; "it is a fine position, with plenty of fresh air." So he alighted just between the feet of the Happy Prince.

"I have a golden bedroom," he said softly to himself as he looked

準備睡覺，正當燕子把頭埋進翅膀底下，忽然有一滴大大的水珠落到身上。「這也太奇怪了！」他嚷嚷道：「天上一朵雲也沒有，星星也清晰明亮，卻下起雨來。北歐的天氣實在討厭。以前蘆葦倒是喜歡雨，但那只是因為她自私罷了。」

接著又一滴水珠落下。

「雕像要是不能擋雨，那還有什麼用？」他說：「我得找個妥當一點的煙囪管帽。」他決定飛離此地。

然而尚未張開翅膀，又落下第三滴水，他抬頭望去，看見了……哎呀！他看見什麼了？

快樂王子淚眼汪汪，淚水沿著他的金色臉頰滑落。他的臉龐在月光下美麗無比，小燕子不禁滿心同情。

「你是誰？」他問道。

「我是快樂王子。」

「那你為什麼哭呢？」燕子問：「把我淋得濕答答的。」

「當我還活著，有一顆人心的時候，」雕像回答：「我不知道什麼是眼淚，因為我住在禁止憂傷進入的無憂宮。白天，我和同伴在花園玩耍；晚上，我在大廳帶領眾人起舞。花園四周有一道高聳的圍牆，但我從來沒想要問問牆外有些什麼，我周遭的一切都是這麼美好。臣子們喊我快樂王子，如果玩樂就是快樂的話，我的確很快樂。我

round, and he prepared to go to sleep; but just as he was putting his head under his wing a large drop of water fell on him. "What a curious thing!" he cried; "there is not a single cloud in the sky, the stars are quite clear and bright, and yet it is raining. The climate in the north of Europe is really dreadful. The Reed used to like the rain, but that was merely her selfishness."

Then another drop fell.

"What is the use of a statue if it cannot keep the rain off?" he said; "I must look for a good chimney-pot," and he determined to fly away.

But before he had opened his wings, a third drop fell, and he looked up, and saw—Ah! what did he see?

The eyes of the Happy Prince were filled with tears, and tears were running down his golden cheeks. His face was so beautiful in the moonlight that the little Swallow was filled with pity.

"Who are you?" he said.

"I am the Happy Prince."

"Why are you weeping then?" asked the Swallow; "you have quite drenched me."

"When I was alive and had a human heart," answered the statue, "I did not know what tears were, for I lived in the Palace of Sans-Souci, where sorrow is not allowed to enter. In the daytime I played with my companions in the garden, and in the evening I led the dance in the Great Hall. Round the garden ran a very lofty wall, but I never cared to ask what lay beyond it, everything about me was so beautiful. My courtiers called me the Happy Prince, and happy indeed I was, if

就這樣活著、這樣死去。我死了以後，他們把我高高地豎在這裡，讓我得以看盡全城的醜陋和苦難，雖然我的心是鉛做的，卻也只能傷心掉淚。」

「什麼！他不是純金的？」燕子心中暗忖。他很有教養，不會大聲議論別人。

「在很遠很遠的地方，」雕像繼續用低沉悅耳的聲音說：「在一條小街上有一戶窮苦人家。其中一扇窗開著，我可以看見一個婦人坐在桌邊。她的臉消瘦憔悴，一雙手被針扎得粗糙發紅，因為她是個裁縫。她正在一件緞面禮服上繡著西番蓮圖案，準備給皇后身邊最美的宮女在下次的宮廷舞會上穿。而她兒子病著躺在房間角落的床上。他正在發燒，說想要吃柳橙，母親卻只能給他河水喝，所以他在哭泣。燕子啊燕子，小燕子，你能不能把我劍柄上的紅寶石送去給她呢？我的腳被固定在這個基座上動不了。」

「大家都在埃及等我，」燕子說：「我的朋友們正沿著尼羅河飛來飛去，和大大的蓮花談天。不久他們就會去睡在偉大國王的墓裡。國王本人躺在一具彩繪棺木中，身上裹著黃色亞麻布，還塗敷了防腐香料。他脖子上掛著一條淺綠色翡翠項鍊，雙手有如枯葉。」

「燕子啊燕子，小燕子，」王子說：「你能不能留下來陪我一晚，當我的信差呢？那個男孩是那麼口渴，他母親又是那麼悲傷。」

pleasure be happiness. So I lived, and so I died. And now that I am dead they have set me up here so high that I can see all the ugliness and all the misery of my city, and though my heart is made of lead yet I cannot chose but weep."

"What! is he not solid gold?" said the Swallow to himself. He was too polite to make any personal remarks out loud.

"Far away," continued the statue in a low musical voice, "far away in a little street there is a poor house. One of the windows is open, and through it I can see a woman seated at a table. Her face is thin and worn, and she has coarse, red hands, all pricked by the needle, for she is a seamstress. She is embroidering passion-flowers on a satin gown for the loveliest of the Queen's maids-of-honour to wear at the next Court-ball. In a bed in the corner of the room her little boy is lying ill. He has a fever, and is asking for oranges. His mother has nothing to give him but river water, so he is crying. Swallow, Swallow, little Swallow, will you not bring her the ruby out of my sword-hilt? My feet are fastened to this pedestal and I cannot move."

"I am waited for in Egypt," said the Swallow. "My friends are flying up and down the Nile, and talking to the large lotus-flowers. Soon they will go to sleep in the tomb of the great King. The King is there himself in his painted coffin. He is wrapped in yellow linen, and embalmed with spices. Round his neck is a chain of pale green jade, and his hands are like withered leaves."

"Swallow, Swallow, little Swallow," said the Prince, "will you not stay with me for one night, and be my messenger? The boy is so thirsty, and the mother so sad."

「我不太喜歡小男生。」燕子回答:「去年夏天我待在河上的時候,有兩個野孩子,他們是磨坊主人的兒子,老是拿石頭丟我。當然了,他們從來沒丟中,我們燕子的飛行技巧太好了,簡簡單單就能避開,再說,我出身的家族也以靈巧聞名,但這種行為實在太不尊重人。」

可是快樂王子滿臉哀傷,讓小燕子心有不忍。「這裡好冷,」他說:「不過我就留下來陪你一晚,當你的信差。」

「謝謝你,小燕子。」王子說。

於是燕子啄出王子劍上的大紅寶石,啣在嘴裡,飛越城裡的屋頂。

他經過了雕著白色大理石天使雕像的大教堂,經過了皇宮,聽見舞會上的樂聲。有位美麗少女和情人來到外面的陽台。「多美妙的星星啊,」他對她說道:「多美妙的愛情魔力啊!」

「希望我的禮服來得及在舞會前做好。」她如此回應:「我還特別吩咐裁縫要繡上西番蓮,不過那些女裁縫都懶得很。」

燕子飛越河上,看見船隻桅杆上掛著燈籠。他飛越猶太街區,看見幾個猶太老人在討價還價,一面用銅秤量著錢幣。最後他來到那戶窮人家,往內一看,只見男孩因為發燒在床上翻來覆去,母親則是累得睡著了。他蹦跳進去,將紅寶石擱在桌上的頂針旁,然後輕輕繞著床飛,用

"I don't think I like boys," answered the Swallow. "Last summer, when I was staying on the river, there were two rude boys, the miller's sons, who were always throwing stones at me. They never hit me, of course; we swallows fly far too well for that, and besides, I come of a family famous for its agility; but still, it was a mark of disrespect."

But the Happy Prince looked so sad that the little Swallow was sorry. "It is very cold here," he said; "but I will stay with you for one night, and be your messenger."

"Thank you, little Swallow," said the Prince.

So the Swallow picked out the great ruby from the Prince's sword, and flew away with it in his beak over the roofs of the town.

He passed by the cathedral tower, where the white marble angels were sculptured. He passed by the palace and heard the sound of dancing. A beautiful girl came out on the balcony with her lover. "How wonderful the stars are," he said to her, "and how wonderful is the power of love!"

"I hope my dress will be ready in time for the State-ball," she answered; "I have ordered passion-flowers to be embroidered on it; but the seamstresses are so lazy."

He passed over the river, and saw the lanterns hanging to the masts of the ships. He passed over the Ghetto, and saw the old Jews bargaining with each other, and weighing out money in copper scales. At last he came to the poor house and looked in. The boy was tossing feverishly on his bed, and the mother had fallen asleep, she was so tired. In he hopped, and laid the great ruby on the table beside the woman's thimble. Then he flew gently round the bed, fanning the

翅膀往小男孩的額頭搧風。「我覺得好涼快！」男孩說：「一定是快好了。」說完便沉沉睡去，睡得又香又甜。

隨後燕子飛回到快樂王子身邊，將事情經過告訴他。「真奇怪，」他說道：「天氣雖然這麼冷，我現在卻覺得挺暖和的。」

「那是因為你做了好事。」王子說。小燕子剛要開始思考，就睡著了。他每次一動腦筋就發睏。

天亮後他飛往河邊洗了個澡。「真是奇景啊！」正在過橋的鳥類學教授說道：「冬天竟然有燕子！」他針對此事給當地報社寫了封長信。每個人都引述信中內容，因為裡面有太多他們不懂的詞彙。

「今晚我要去埃及了，」燕子一想到就興奮無比。他造訪了所有的公共紀念建築，還在教堂尖塔頂端歇了大半天。他所到之處，麻雀都嘰嘰喳喳地互相傳告：「好特別的陌生人啊！」燕子感到十分愉快。

月亮升起時，他飛回到快樂王子身邊，高喊道：「你想託我在埃及做什麼嗎？我就要出發了。」

「燕子啊燕子，小燕子，」王子說：「你能不能再多陪我一晚？」

「大家在埃及等我呢，」燕子回答：「明天我的朋友們就會飛往尼羅河第二道瀑布。那裡有河馬躺臥在香蒲間，有門農神像端坐在巨大的花崗岩寶座上。他整夜守望

boy's forehead with his wings. "How cool I feel," said the boy, "I must be getting better"; and he sank into a delicious slumber.

Then the Swallow flew back to the Happy Prince, and told him what he had done. "It is curious," he remarked, "but I feel quite warm now, although it is so cold."

"That is because you have done a good action," said the Prince. And the little Swallow began to think, and then he fell asleep. Thinking always made him sleepy.

When day broke he flew down to the river and had a bath. "What a remarkable phenomenon," said the Professor of Ornithology as he was passing over the bridge. "A swallow in winter!" And he wrote a long letter about it to the local newspaper. Every one quoted it, it was full of so many words that they could not understand.

"To-night I go to Egypt," said the Swallow, and he was in high spirits at the prospect. He visited all the public monuments, and sat a long time on top of the church steeple. Wherever he went the Sparrows chirruped, and said to each other, "What a distinguished stranger!" so he enjoyed himself very much.

When the moon rose he flew back to the Happy Prince. "Have you any commissions for Egypt?" he cried; "I am just starting."

"Swallow, Swallow, little Swallow," said the Prince, "will you not stay with me one night longer?"

"I am waited for in Egypt," answered the Swallow. "To-morrow my friends will fly up to the Second Cataract. The river-horse couches there among the bulrushes, and on a great granite throne sits the God Memnon. All night long he watches the stars, and when the morning

著星星，當晨星一亮，他便發出一聲喜悅的歡呼，然後又沉默下來。到了中午，黃色獅群會來到河邊喝水，他們的眼睛像綠寶石一樣，吼聲比嘩嘩的瀑布聲還要響亮。」

「燕子啊燕子，小燕子，」王子說：「在城市遙遠的那一端，我看見一個小閣樓裡，有個年輕人伏在堆滿紙張的案前，一旁有個玻璃杯，裡面擺著一束枯萎的紫羅蘭。他有一頭棕色小捲髮，嘴唇紅如石榴，眼睛大而迷濛。他正在努力完成劇本要交給劇場經理，但實在冷得寫不下去。爐架裡沒有生火，他也餓得頭昏眼花。」

「我就再多陪你一晚吧。」燕子說，他確實有副好心腸。「你要我再送一顆紅寶石去給他嗎？」

「唉！我已經沒有紅寶石了。」王子說：「我現在只剩一對眼睛，是用千年前從印度運出來的稀有藍寶石做成的。你就啄出其中一顆送去給他吧。他可以賣給珠寶商，然後買點柴火取暖，把劇本寫完。」

「親愛的王子，我做不到。」燕子說著哭了起來。

「燕子啊燕子，小燕子，」王子說：「請照我說的做吧。」

於是燕子啄出王子的眼睛，飛往學生住的閣樓。進屋並不困難，因為屋頂破了個洞。他從洞口疾飛而入，年輕人雙手抱頭，沒聽見鳥的鼓翅聲，後來一抬頭，才忽然發現枯萎的紫羅蘭上躺著一顆美麗的藍寶石。

star shines he utters one cry of joy, and then he is silent. At noon the yellow lions come down to the water's edge to drink. They have eyes like green beryls, and their roar is louder than the roar of the cataract."

"Swallow, Swallow, little Swallow," said the Prince, "far away across the city I see a young man in a garret. He is leaning over a desk covered with papers, and in a tumbler by his side there is a bunch of withered violets. His hair is brown and crisp, and his lips are red as a pomegranate, and he has large and dreamy eyes. He is trying to finish a play for the Director of the Theatre, but he is too cold to write any more. There is no fire in the grate, and hunger has made him faint."

"I will wait with you one night longer," said the Swallow, who really had a good heart. "Shall I take him another ruby?"

"Alas! I have no ruby now," said the Prince; "my eyes are all that I have left. They are made of rare sapphires, which were brought out of India a thousand years ago. Pluck out one of them and take it to him. He will sell it to the jeweller, and buy food and firewood, and finish his play."

"Dear Prince," said the Swallow, "I cannot do that"; and he began to weep.

"Swallow, Swallow, little Swallow," said the Prince, "do as I command you."

So the Swallow plucked out the Prince's eye, and flew away to the student's garret. It was easy enough to get in, as there was a hole in the roof. Through this he darted, and came into the room. The young man had his head buried in his hands, so he did not hear the flutter of the bird's wings, and when he looked up he found the beautiful

「我終於受到賞識了！」他大喊道：「這一定是某個伯樂送的。現在我可以完成劇本了。」他顯得高興萬分。

翌日，燕子飛到港口，棲在一艘大船的桅杆上，看著水手用繩索將一口口大箱子拉出船艙。「嘿嘿嗬！」每拉起一只箱子，他們便大喝道。「我要去埃及了！」燕子高喊，卻無人理會，當月亮升起，他便飛回去找快樂王子。

「我是來跟你辭行的。」他喊道。

「燕子啊燕子，小燕子，」王子說：「你能不能再留下來陪我一晚？」

「冬天到了，」燕子回答：「這裡很快就會降下寒冷的冰雪。在埃及，溫暖的陽光照耀著青翠的棕櫚樹，鱷魚趴在泥地裡，懶洋洋地東張西望。我的同伴正在巴貝克神殿裡築巢，粉紅色和白色的鴿子在一旁看著，咕咕叫聲此起彼落。親愛的王子，我真的得走了，但我絕對不會忘記你，明年春天我會帶兩顆美麗寶石回來，替補你送人的那兩顆。我的紅寶石將會比紅玫瑰還紅艷，藍寶石會像大海一樣湛藍。」

「底下的廣場上，」快樂王子說：「站著一個賣火柴的小女孩。她不小心把火柴掉進水溝裡，火柴全毀了。她要是沒帶點錢回家，就會挨父親打，所以她在哭。她腳上沒穿鞋襪，小小的頭上也沒戴帽子。你啄出我另一隻眼睛送去給她，那麼她父親就不會打她了。」

sapphire lying on the withered violets.

"I am beginning to be appreciated," he cried; "this is from some great admirer. Now I can finish my play," and he looked quite happy.

The next day the Swallow flew down to the harbour. He sat on the mast of a large vessel and watched the sailors hauling big chests out of the hold with ropes. "Heave a-hoy!" they shouted as each chest came up. "I am going to Egypt"! cried the Swallow, but nobody minded, and when the moon rose he flew back to the Happy Prince.

"I am come to bid you good-bye," he cried.

"Swallow, Swallow, little Swallow," said the Prince, "will you not stay with me one night longer?"

"It is winter," answered the Swallow, "and the chill snow will soon be here. In Egypt the sun is warm on the green palm-trees, and the crocodiles lie in the mud and look lazily about them. My companions are building a nest in the Temple of Baalbec, and the pink and white doves are watching them, and cooing to each other. Dear Prince, I must leave you, but I will never forget you, and next spring I will bring you back two beautiful jewels in place of those you have given away. The ruby shall be redder than a red rose, and the sapphire shall be as blue as the great sea."

"In the square below," said the Happy Prince, "there stands a little match-girl. She has let her matches fall in the gutter, and they are all spoiled. Her father will beat her if she does not bring home some money, and she is crying. She has no shoes or stockings, and her little head is bare. Pluck out my other eye, and give it to her, and her father will not beat her."

「我可以留下來再陪你一晚，」燕子說：「但我不能啄你那隻眼睛，不然你就全瞎了。」

「燕子啊燕子，小燕子，」王子說：「照我說的做吧。」

於是他啄出王子的另一眼，啣著它疾飛而下，驀地飛到賣火柴的女孩身邊，讓寶石輕巧地掉落在她掌心。「好漂亮的玻璃珠啊！」小女孩大叫，然後笑著跑回家去。

燕子隨即回到王子身旁。「你現在看不見了，」他說：「我要永遠陪在你身邊。」

「不，小燕子。」可憐的王子說：「你一定得去埃及。」

「我要永遠陪在你身邊。」燕子說完便在王子的腳邊睡下。

隔天一整天他都棲坐在王子肩上，說一些他在異國的見聞給王子聽。他說到紅色朱鷺排成長列站在尼羅河畔，嘴裡叼著金魚；說到獅身人面的司芬克斯，從開天闢地以來就一直住在沙漠裡，無所不知、無所不曉；說到商人緩緩傍著駱駝行進，手中握著琥珀串珠；說到月亮山之王，黑如烏木，會膜拜一顆大水晶；說到一條睡在棕櫚樹上的大青蛇，有二十個祭司拿蜂蜜蛋糕餵牠；說到一群侏儒乘著扁平的大樹葉，橫跨一座大湖，並不停地與蝴蝶開戰。

「親愛的小燕子，」王子說：「你告訴我的這些事令

"I will stay with you one night longer," said the Swallow, "but I cannot pluck out your eye. You would be quite blind then."

"Swallow, Swallow, little Swallow," said the Prince, "do as I command you."

So he plucked out the Prince's other eye, and darted down with it. He swooped past the match-girl, and slipped the jewel into the palm of her hand. "What a lovely bit of glass," cried the little girl; and she ran home, laughing.

Then the Swallow came back to the Prince. "You are blind now," he said, "so I will stay with you always."

"No, little Swallow," said the poor Prince, "you must go away to Egypt."

"I will stay with you always," said the Swallow, and he slept at the Prince's feet.

All the next day he sat on the Prince's shoulder, and told him stories of what he had seen in strange lands. He told him of the red ibises, who stand in long rows on the banks of the Nile, and catch gold-fish in their beaks; of the Sphinx, who is as old as the world itself, and lives in the desert, and knows everything; of the merchants, who walk slowly by the side of their camels, and carry amber beads in their hands; of the King of the Mountains of the Moon, who is as black as ebony, and worships a large crystal; of the great green snake that sleeps in a palm-tree, and has twenty priests to feed it with honey-cakes; and of the pygmies who sail over a big lake on large flat leaves, and are always at war with the butterflies.

"Dear little Swallow," said the Prince, "you tell me of marvellous

人驚嘆，但最令人驚嘆的莫過於世間男女的痛苦，人世間最大的謎莫過於苦難了。小燕子，飛到我的城市上空去吧，告訴我你看見了些什麼。」

於是燕子飛到城市上空，看見富人在華宅裡嬉笑作樂，大門口卻坐著乞丐。他飛入暗巷，看見飢餓的孩子們蒼白著臉，無精打采地望向幽暗街道。一座拱橋下，有兩名小男孩互相摟著取暖。「好餓啊！」他們說。「你們不許躺在這裡。」巡守人嚷嚷道，男孩們於是漫無目的地走進雨中。

接著，燕子飛了回去，將所見的情景告訴王子。

「我全身都是純金箔片，」王子說：「你就一片一片取下來，送給我貧窮的子民吧。世人總覺得有黃金就很快樂。」

燕子將金箔一片片叼下，直到快樂王子變得單調灰暗。他將金箔一片片送到窮人手上，孩子們的臉漸顯紅潤，成群笑著在街上玩耍。「我們現在有麵包吃了！」他們歡呼道。

接著，城裡下雪了，寒霜隨之而來。街道彷彿白銀打造而成，一片亮晶晶，長長的冰柱猶如一支支水晶匕首垂掛在屋簷下，在外走動的人全都穿著皮衣，小男孩也都戴上大紅帽，在冰面上溜著冰。

可憐的小燕子愈來愈冷，但因為實在太愛王子而不肯

things, but more marvellous than anything is the suffering of men and of women. There is no Mystery so great as Misery. Fly over my city, little Swallow, and tell me what you see there."

So the Swallow flew over the great city, and saw the rich making merry in their beautiful houses, while the beggars were sitting at the gates. He flew into dark lanes, and saw the white faces of starving children looking out listlessly at the black streets. Under the archway of a bridge two little boys were lying in one another's arms to try and keep themselves warm. "How hungry we are!" they said. "You must not lie here," shouted the Watchman, and they wandered out into the rain.

Then he flew back and told the Prince what he had seen.

"I am covered with fine gold," said the Prince, "you must take it off, leaf by leaf, and give it to my poor; the living always think that gold can make them happy."

Leaf after leaf of the fine gold the Swallow picked off, till the Happy Prince looked quite dull and grey. Leaf after leaf of the fine gold he brought to the poor, and the children's faces grew rosier, and they laughed and played games in the street. "We have bread now!" they cried.

Then the snow came, and after the snow came the frost. The streets looked as if they were made of silver, they were so bright and glistening; long icicles like crystal daggers hung down from the eaves of the houses, everybody went about in furs, and the little boys wore scarlet caps and skated on the ice.

The poor little Swallow grew colder and colder, but he would not

離開。他趁著麵包師傅不注意，啄食店門外的麵包屑，並不停鼓翅取暖。

然而到了最後，他知道自己就要死了，僅剩一點力氣能最後再一次飛到王子肩頭。「再見了，親愛的王子！」他低聲說：「可以讓我親親你的手嗎？」

「很高興你終於要去埃及了，小燕子。」王子說：「你已經待得太久，不過你得親吻我的嘴，因為我愛你。」

「我不是要去埃及，」燕子說：「而是要去死亡之家。死亡是睡眠的兄弟，不是嗎？」

他說完親了親快樂王子的嘴，便跌落在他腳邊死去。

同一時間，雕像內部響起奇怪的劈啪聲，像是什麼東西碎了。原來王子那顆鉛做的心突然一裂為二，肯定是寒霜逼人太甚呀。

次日一早，市長在幾位議員陪同下走進下方的廣場。經過圓柱時，他抬頭看著雕像說：「老天哪！快樂王子怎麼這麼一副寒酸相！」

「可不是嘛，真寒酸！」向來附和市長的議員們齊聲高喊，並走上前細看。

「他劍上的紅寶石掉了，眼睛不見了，身上也不再金光閃閃。」市長說：「老實說，他比乞丐好不了多少！」

「比乞丐好不了多少。」議員們應和。

leave the Prince, he loved him too well. He picked up crumbs outside the baker's door when the baker was not looking and tried to keep himself warm by flapping his wings.

But at last he knew that he was going to die. He had just strength to fly up to the Prince's shoulder once more. "Good-bye, dear Prince!" he murmured, "will you let me kiss your hand?"

"I am glad that you are going to Egypt at last, little Swallow," said the Prince, "you have stayed too long here; but you must kiss me on the lips, for I love you."

"It is not to Egypt that I am going," said the Swallow. "I am going to the House of Death. Death is the brother of Sleep, is he not?"

And he kissed the Happy Prince on the lips, and fell down dead at his feet.

At that moment a curious crack sounded inside the statue, as if something had broken. The fact is that the leaden heart had snapped right in two. It certainly was a dreadfully hard frost.

Early the next morning the Mayor was walking in the square below in company with the Town Councillors. As they passed the column he looked up at the statue: "Dear me! how shabby the Happy Prince looks!" he said.

"How shabby indeed!" cried the Town Councillors, who always agreed with the Mayor; and they went up to look at it.

"The ruby has fallen out of his sword, his eyes are gone, and he is golden no longer," said the Mayor in fact, "he is little better than a beggar!"

"Little better than a beggar," said the Town Councillors.

「他腳邊還死了一隻鳥！」市長接著說：「我們真該發布公告，不允許任何鳥死在這裡。」書記官立刻記下這項建議。

　　於是他們拆除了快樂王子雕像。「既然他不再美麗，也就不再有用了。」大學的藝術系教授如此說。

　　然後雕像被丟進火爐熔化，市長則召開市政會議，以決定金屬的用途。「當然得再塑造一尊雕像了，」他說：「那就立我的雕像吧。」

　　「我的！」每位市議員都這麼說，結果吵了起來。據我最後聽說的消息，他們依然爭吵不休。

　　「這可真是奇怪了！」鑄造廠的工頭說：「這顆破裂的鉛心竟然熔化不了，只好把它丟掉了。」於是他們把它丟進垃圾堆，死去的燕子剛好也躺在那裡。

　　「你到城裡去替我找來兩件最寶貴的東西。」上帝對一位天使說，結果天使帶來了那顆鉛做的心和死去的燕子。

　　「選得好，」上帝說：「這隻小鳥將永遠在我的天堂花園裡鳴唱，而快樂王子將在我的黃金城裡讚頌我。」

"And here is actually a dead bird at his feet!" continued the Mayor. "We must really issue a proclamation that birds are not to be allowed to die here." And the Town Clerk made a note of the suggestion.

So they pulled down the statue of the Happy Prince. "As he is no longer beautiful he is no longer useful," said the Art Professor at the University.

Then they melted the statue in a furnace, and the Mayor held a meeting of the Corporation to decide what was to be done with the metal. "We must have another statue, of course," he said, "and it shall be a statue of myself."

"Of myself," said each of the Town Councillors, and they quarrelled. When I last heard of them they were quarrelling still.

"What a strange thing!" said the overseer of the workmen at the foundry. "This broken lead heart will not melt in the furnace. We must throw it away." So they threw it on a dust-heap where the dead Swallow was also lying.

"Bring me the two most precious things in the city," said God to one of His Angels; and the Angel brought Him the leaden heart and the dead bird.

"You have rightly chosen," said God, "for in my garden of Paradise this little bird shall sing for evermore, and in my city of gold the Happy Prince shall praise me."

夜鶯與玫瑰

The Nightingale and the Rose

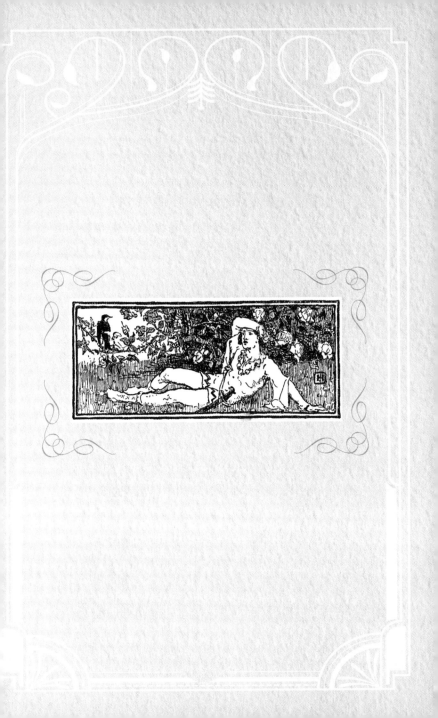

「**她**說只要我送她紅玫瑰，她就願意與我共舞。」年輕學生呼喊道：「可是我整個花園裡沒有一朵紅玫瑰。」

夜鶯從冬青櫟樹上的巢中聽見他說話，心下好奇，便透過枝葉縫隙往外看。

「我整個花園都沒有紅玫瑰！」他吶喊著，美麗的眼中充滿淚水。「呵，幸福之所繫竟是如此渺小的事物！我讀遍聖賢書，通曉所有哲學奧祕，卻只因為少了一朵紅玫瑰，而使人生變得如此悲慘。」

「愛情的忠實信徒終於出現了，」夜鶯說：「雖然不認識他，但我夜復一夜為他歌頌，我夜復一夜對群星述說他的故事，如今總算見到他了。他的頭髮深暗如風信子花，嘴唇鮮紅如他渴望的玫瑰，但他的臉卻因激情而蒼白如象牙，眉頭因憂愁而深鎖。」

「明天晚上王子要舉辦舞會，」年輕學生喃喃自語：「我的意中人也會參加。如果我送她一朵紅玫瑰，她便會與我共舞到天明。如果我送她一朵紅玫瑰，我便能將她擁在懷裡，她會將頭倚在我肩上，讓我牢牢握著她的手。可是我的花園裡沒有紅玫瑰，我只能孤獨枯坐，與她失之交臂。她將無視我的存在，我也將因此心碎。」

「他果然是愛情的忠實信徒，」夜鶯說：「我所歌頌的，折磨著他，令我感到喜悅的，卻是他的痛苦。愛情可真是神奇。它比綠寶石更寶貴，比上等貓眼石更值得珍

"She said that she would dance with me if I brought her red roses," cried the young Student; "but in all my garden there is no red rose."

From her nest in the holm-oak tree the Nightingale heard him, and she looked out through the leaves, and wondered.

"No red rose in all my garden!" he cried, and his beautiful eyes filled with tears. "Ah, on what little things does happiness depend! I have read all that the wise men have written, and all the secrets of philosophy are mine, yet for want of a red rose is my life made wretched."

"Here at last is a true lover," said the Nightingale. "Night after night have I sung of him, though I knew him not: night after night have I told his story to the stars, and now I see him. His hair is dark as the hyacinth-blossom, and his lips are red as the rose of his desire; but passion has made his face like pale ivory, and sorrow has set her seal upon his brow."

"The Prince gives a ball to-morrow night," murmured the young Student, "and my love will be of the company. If I bring her a red rose she will dance with me till dawn. If I bring her a red rose, I shall hold her in my arms, and she will lean her head upon my shoulder, and her hand will be clasped in mine. But there is no red rose in my garden, so I shall sit lonely, and she will pass me by. She will have no heed of me, and my heart will break."

"Here indeed is the true lover," said the Nightingale. "What I sing of, he suffers—what is joy to me, to him is pain. Surely Love is a wonderful thing. It is more precious than emeralds, and dearer than

惜，用珍珠和石榴買不到，市場也不見上架，不能向商人購買，也無法用秤量黃金的天秤計算。」

「樂師們會入席就坐，」年輕學生說：「彈奏弦樂，我的意中人會隨著豎琴與小提琴的音樂起舞，舞姿翩翩、足不點地，身穿華服的臣子會蜂擁而上將她環繞。但她不會與我共舞，因為我沒有送她紅玫瑰。」話畢，他猛然撲倒在草地上，雙手掩面，痛哭失聲。

「他為什麼哭呢？」小綠蜥問道，他揚起尾巴，從學生身邊跑過。

「就是啊，為什麼呢？」正追著一線日光飛來飛去的蝴蝶說道。

「就是啊，為什麼呢？」一朵雛菊小聲地問隔壁同伴，聲音又輕又細。

「他是為了一朵紅玫瑰而哭。」夜鶯說。

「為了紅玫瑰？」大夥驚呼道：「真是太荒謬了！」那隻有點玩世不恭的小蜥蜴，立刻大笑出聲。

但夜鶯了解學生憂傷的祕密，便默默棲在櫟樹上，思索愛情的奧祕。

突然間她展開棕色翅膀，翱翔高飛，如影子般掠過樹叢，又如影子般飛過花園。

草坪正中央坐落著一叢美麗的玫瑰，她一見立即飛過

fine opals. Pearls and pomegranates cannot buy it, nor is it set forth in the marketplace. It may not be purchased of the merchants, nor can it be weighed out in the balance for gold."

"The musicians will sit in their gallery," said the young Student, "and play upon their stringed instruments, and my love will dance to the sound of the harp and the violin. She will dance so lightly that her feet will not touch the floor, and the courtiers in their gay dresses will throng round her. But with me she will not dance, for I have no red rose to give her"; and he flung himself down on the grass, and buried his face in his hands, and wept.

"Why is he weeping?" asked a little Green Lizard, as he ran past him with his tail in the air.

"Why, indeed?" said a Butterfly, who was fluttering about after a sunbeam.

"Why, indeed?" whispered a Daisy to his neighbour, in a soft, low voice.

"He is weeping for a red rose," said the Nightingale.

"For a red rose?" they cried; "how very ridiculous!" and the little Lizard, who was something of a cynic, laughed outright.

But the Nightingale understood the secret of the Student's sorrow, and she sat silent in the oak-tree, and thought about the mystery of Love.

Suddenly she spread her brown wings for flight, and soared into the air. She passed through the grove like a shadow, and like a shadow she sailed across the garden.

In the centre of the grass-plot was standing a beautiful Rose-tree,

去，棲落在一根小枝上。

「給我一朵紅玫瑰，」她喊著說：「我會為你唱最動聽的歌。」

但樹叢搖搖頭回答道：「我的玫瑰是白色的，白得宛如海中泡沫，白得更勝山頭積雪。不過我有個兄弟長在舊日晷附近，你去找他吧，也許他能實現你的願望。」

於是夜鶯飛往舊日晷附近的那叢玫瑰。

「給我一朵紅玫瑰，」她高喊：「我會為你唱最動聽的歌。」

但樹叢還是搖頭，回答道：「我的玫瑰是黃色的，黃得宛如琥珀寶座上美人魚的秀髮，黃得更勝刈草人帶著鐮刀來收割前草原上盛開的水仙。不過我有個兄弟長在那個學生的窗下，你去找他吧，也許他能如你所願。」

於是夜鶯飛往學生窗下的那叢玫瑰。

「給我一朵紅玫瑰，」她高喊：「我會為你唱最動聽的歌。」

不料，樹叢依然搖頭。

「我的玫瑰是紅色的，」它回答道：「紅得宛如鴿子腳，紅得更勝海洋洞穴中隨浪不停擺動的大片扇狀珊瑚。只可惜寒冬凍結了我的血管，嚴霜凍傷了我的花苞，暴風

and when she saw it she flew over to it, and lit upon a spray.

"Give me a red rose," she cried, "and I will sing you my sweetest song."

But the Tree shook its head.

"My roses are white," it answered; "as white as the foam of the sea, and whiter than the snow upon the mountain. But go to my brother who grows round the old sun-dial, and perhaps he will give you what you want."

So the Nightingale flew over to the Rose-tree that was growing round the old sun-dial.

"Give me a red rose," she cried, "and I will sing you my sweetest song."

But the Tree shook its head.

"My roses are yellow," it answered; "as yellow as the hair of the mermaiden who sits upon an amber throne, and yellower than the daffodil that blooms in the meadow before the mower comes with his scythe. But go to my brother who grows beneath the Student's window, and perhaps he will give you what you want."

So the Nightingale flew over to the Rose-tree that was growing beneath the Student's window.

"Give me a red rose," she cried, "and I will sing you my sweetest song."

But the Tree shook its head.

"My roses are red," it answered, "as red as the feet of the dove, and redder than the great fans of coral that wave and wave in the ocean-cavern. But the winter has chilled my veins, and the frost has nipped

雪折斷了我的枝枒，今年我一朵玫瑰也開不出來。」

「我只要一朵紅玫瑰，」夜鶯喊道：「只要一朵紅玫瑰呀！難道就沒有辦法讓我如願嗎？」

「辦法倒是有，」樹叢回答：「但太可怕了，我不敢告訴你。」

「告訴我吧，我不怕。」夜鶯說。

「你若想要紅玫瑰，」樹叢說：「就得在月光下用音樂打造，用你自己的心頭血來染紅。你必須將胸口抵著棘刺，對我唱一整夜的歌，棘刺要穿透你的心臟，讓血流進我的血管，成為我的生命泉源。」

「犧牲生命換取一朵玫瑰，代價未免太高了。」夜鶯高喊：「所有人的生命都很寶貴。棲於蒼翠林間，看著太陽駕馭金黃馬車、月亮駕馭珍珠馬車，是何等樂事。山楂的氣味芳香可人，隱藏在山谷裡的藍鐘花，和山丘上隨風飄揚的石楠花也同樣可人。不過愛情比生命更美好，何況比起人的心，鳥兒的心又算得了什麼？」

於是她展開棕色翅膀，翱翔高飛，如影子般掠過花園，又如影子般飛過樹叢。

那個年輕學生還像她離開時一樣躺在草地上，美麗眼中的淚水也還沒乾。

「快樂一點，」夜鶯高啼：「快樂一點，你會得到你的紅玫瑰。我會在月光下用音樂打造它，用我自己的心頭

my buds, and the storm has broken my branches, and I shall have no roses at all this year."

"One red rose is all I want," cried the Nightingale, "only one red rose! Is there no way by which I can get it?"

"There is a way," answered the Tree; "but it is so terrible that I dare not tell it to you."

"Tell it to me," said the Nightingale, "I am not afraid."

"If you want a red rose," said the Tree, "you must build it out of music by moonlight, and stain it with your own heart's-blood. You must sing to me with your breast against a thorn. All night long you must sing to me, and the thorn must pierce your heart, and your life-blood must flow into my veins, and become mine."

"Death is a great price to pay for a red rose," cried the Nightingale, "and Life is very dear to all. It is pleasant to sit in the green wood, and to watch the Sun in his chariot of gold, and the Moon in her chariot of pearl. Sweet is the scent of the hawthorn, and sweet are the bluebells that hide in the valley, and the heather that blows on the hill. Yet Love is better than Life, and what is the heart of a bird compared to the heart of a man?"

So she spread her brown wings for flight, and soared into the air. She swept over the garden like a shadow, and like a shadow she sailed through the grove.

The young Student was still lying on the grass, where she had left him, and the tears were not yet dry in his beautiful eyes.

"Be happy," cried the Nightingale, "be happy; you shall have your red rose. I will build it out of music by moonlight, and stain it with my

血將它染紅。我唯一要求的回報就是你必須當愛情的忠實信徒，因為儘管哲學聰明，愛情比它更聰明；儘管權勢強大，愛情比它更強大。愛情的翅膀火紅如焰，身體如焰般火紅，嘴唇香甜如蜜，氣息好似乳香。」

學生從草地上仰起頭，側耳傾聽，卻聽不懂夜鶯在說什麼，因為他只懂得書中文字。

但櫟樹聽懂了，心中感傷，因為他非常喜歡這隻在他枝葉間築巢的小夜鶯。

「最後再為我唱一曲吧。」櫟樹輕聲說：「你走了我會覺得寂寞。」

於是夜鶯為櫟樹歌唱，嗓音猶如銀罐流出的淙淙水聲。

她唱完歌後，學生站起身，從口袋掏出一本筆記和一枝鉛筆。

「她技巧不錯，」他從樹叢間走開，一面自言自語：「這點無可否認，可是有感情嗎？恐怕沒有。事實上，她和大多數藝術家一樣，完全只重形式而沒有一點真心。她不會為他人犧牲自己，她一心只想著音樂，而大家都知道藝術是自私的。但話說回來，你不得不承認她的嗓音裡不乏美妙音色，只可惜這些音色毫無意義，也全然無用！」他走進房間，躺到乾草鋪的小床上，開始想起心上人來，不一會兒便睡著了。

當月光照亮天穹，夜鶯飛到玫瑰樹叢前，讓棘刺刺進

own heart's-blood. All that I ask of you in return is that you will be a true lover, for Love is wiser than Philosophy, though she is wise, and mightier than Power, though he is mighty. Flame-coloured are his wings, and coloured like flame is his body. His lips are sweet as honey, and his breath is like frankincense."

The Student looked up from the grass, and listened, but he could not understand what the Nightingale was saying to him, for he only knew the things that are written down in books.

But the Oak-tree understood, and felt sad, for he was very fond of the little Nightingale who had built her nest in his branches.

"Sing me one last song," he whispered; "I shall feel very lonely when you are gone."

So the Nightingale sang to the Oak-tree, and her voice was like water bubbling from a silver jar.

When she had finished her song the Student got up, and pulled a note-book and a lead-pencil out of his pocket.

"She has form," he said to himself, as he walked away through the grove—"that cannot be denied to her; but has she got feeling? I am afraid not. In fact, she is like most artists; she is all style, without any sincerity. She would not sacrifice herself for others. She thinks merely of music, and everybody knows that the arts are selfish. Still, it must be admitted that she has some beautiful notes in her voice. What a pity it is that they do not mean anything, or do any practical good." And he went into his room, and lay down on his little pallet-bed, and began to think of his love; and, after a time, he fell asleep.

And when the Moon shone in the heavens the Nightingale flew

胸口。她徹夜啼鳴，胸口始終抵著棘刺，晶瑩剔透的寒月也傾身聆聽。她徹夜啼鳴，玫瑰棘刺往胸口愈刺愈深，她的血漸漸流失。

她首先歌頌在男孩與女孩心中萌芽的愛情。隨著歌曲一首接著一首，玫瑰樹叢最頂端的小枝上也一瓣接著一瓣，綻放出一朵奇麗的玫瑰。一開始，花瓣蒼白得宛如輕攏河面的薄霧，宛如晨光末梢，也似黎明的翅膀般銀白。一如銀鏡裡的玫瑰花影，又如水池中的玫瑰花影，綻放在樹叢頂端小枝上的玫瑰便是如此。

但樹叢呼喊著要夜鶯再往棘刺靠緊一點。「小夜鶯，再用力一點。」樹叢喊道：「要不然玫瑰還沒完成天就亮了。」

因此夜鶯更用力地抵住棘刺，歌聲也愈來愈嘹亮，因為她歌頌的是男人與女人靈魂深處萌生的熱情。

這時玫瑰花瓣泛起一抹淡淡的粉紅，就像新郎親吻新娘唇瓣時，臉上泛起的紅暈。但是棘刺尚未戳入她的心，玫瑰花心依然蒼白，因為只有夜鶯心頭的血才能將花心染紅。

樹叢依舊高喊著要夜鶯再往棘刺緊靠。「再用力一點，小夜鶯。」樹叢大喊：「要不然玫瑰還沒完成天就亮了。」

to the Rose-tree, and set her breast against the thorn. All night long she sang with her breast against the thorn, and the cold crystal Moon leaned down and listened. All night long she sang, and the thorn went deeper and deeper into her breast, and her life-blood ebbed away from her.

She sang first of the birth of love in the heart of a boy and a girl. And on the top-most spray of the Rose-tree there blossomed a marvellous rose, petal following petal, as song followed song. Pale was it, at first, as the mist that hangs over the river—pale as the feet of the morning, and silver as the wings of the dawn. As the shadow of a rose in a mirror of silver, as the shadow of a rose in a water-pool, so was the rose that blossomed on the topmost spray of the Tree.

But the Tree cried to the Nightingale to press closer against the thorn. "Press closer, little Nightingale," cried the Tree, "or the Day will come before the rose is finished."

So the Nightingale pressed closer against the thorn, and louder and louder grew her song, for she sang of the birth of passion in the soul of a man and a maid.

And a delicate flush of pink came into the leaves of the rose, like the flush in the face of the bridegroom when he kisses the lips of the bride. But the thorn had not yet reached her heart, so the rose's heart remained white, for only a Nightingale's heart's-blood can crimson the heart of a rose.

And the Tree cried to the Nightingale to press closer against the thorn. "Press closer, little Nightingale," cried the Tree, "or the Day will come before the rose is finished."

於是夜鶯更加用力抵住棘刺，尖刺碰觸到她的心，頓時一陣劇痛竄遍全身。難耐呀，痛楚難耐，但歌聲卻愈來愈狂野，因為她歌頌的是因死亡而趨於完美的愛情、不會葬送在墳墓裡的愛情。

那朵奇麗的玫瑰轉為嫣紅，猶如東方天際的玫瑰紅。圈繞在外的花瓣嫣紅，花心亦如紅寶石般嫣紅。

然而夜鶯的聲音逐漸變得微弱，她開始鼓動小翅膀，一層薄翳覆蓋了雙眼。她的歌聲愈來愈微弱，接著感覺喉嚨好像被什麼梗住。

這時她爆發出最後一段歌聲。白月娘聽見了，一時忘了黎明將至，在天上流連忘返。紅玫瑰聽見了，欣喜若狂渾身打顫，並在寒冷的晨風中綻開花瓣。回音帶著歌聲來到山中的紫色洞穴，喚醒了睡夢中的牧羊人。歌聲飄過河畔的蘆葦叢，蘆葦便將歌聲中的訊息傳達給大海。

「你看，你看！玫瑰已經完成了。」樹叢高喊，但夜鶯沒有應聲，她已躺在長草叢中死去，棘刺還扎在心口。

到了中午，學生打開窗戶往外看。

「哇，真是奇蹟般的幸運，」他大喊：「這裡就有一朵紅玫瑰！我這一生從未見過這樣的玫瑰，這麼美麗，一定有個很長的拉丁學名。」他說著俯身將花摘下。

他隨即戴上帽子，拿著玫瑰跑到教授家。

So the Nightingale pressed closer against the thorn, and the thorn touched her heart, and a fierce pang of pain shot through her. Bitter, bitter was the pain, and wilder and wilder grew her song, for she sang of the Love that is perfected by Death, of the Love that dies not in the tomb.

And the marvellous rose became crimson, like the rose of the eastern sky. Crimson was the girdle of petals, and crimson as a ruby was the heart.

But the Nightingale's voice grew fainter, and her little wings began to beat, and a film came over her eyes. Fainter and fainter grew her song, and she felt something choking her in her throat.

Then she gave one last burst of music. The white Moon heard it, and she forgot the dawn, and lingered on in the sky. The red rose heard it, and it trembled all over with ecstasy, and opened its petals to the cold morning air. Echo bore it to her purple cavern in the hills, and woke the sleeping shepherds from their dreams. It floated through the reeds of the river, and they carried its message to the sea.

"Look, look!" cried the Tree, "the rose is finished now"; but the Nightingale made no answer, for she was lying dead in the long grass, with the thorn in her heart.

And at noon the Student opened his window and looked out.

"Why, what a wonderful piece of luck!" he cried; "here is a red rose! I have never seen any rose like it in all my life. It is so beautiful that I am sure it has a long Latin name"; and he leaned down and plucked it.

Then he put on his hat, and ran up to the Professor's house with

教授的女兒正坐在門口，搖著紡車紡織藍色絲線，小狗趴在她腳邊。

「你說過，只要我送你紅玫瑰，你就會和我跳舞。」學生高喊：「喏，這是全世界最紅的玫瑰，今晚你就把它別在心口上，當我們共舞時，它會告訴你我多麼愛你。」

不料女孩蹙起眉頭。

「這花恐怕和我的禮服不搭。」她回答道：「再說，內務大臣的姪子送了我一些高級珠寶，誰都知道珠寶比花有價值多了。」

「好哇，真沒想到你這麼不識好歹。」學生氣憤地說，然後將玫瑰往街上一丟，花掉進排水溝，被車輪輾了過去。

「不識好歹！」女孩說：「告訴你吧，你才沒教養，說真的，你以為你是誰啊？不就只是個學生。哼，我才不信你跟內務大臣的姪子一樣有銀鞋扣。」她隨即起身進屋。

「愛情真是愚蠢的玩意！」學生邊說邊走開來。「還不及邏輯的一半有用，因為它什麼也證明不了，老是說一些不會發生的事，讓人信以為真。老實說它太不務實了，現今這個年代，務實最重要，我還是回到哲學世界裡研究形而上學吧。」

於是他回到自己房間，拖出一本布滿灰塵的大書，讀了起來。

the rose in his hand.

The daughter of the Professor was sitting in the doorway winding blue silk on a reel, and her little dog was lying at her feet.

"You said that you would dance with me if I brought you a red rose," cried the Student. "Here is the reddest rose in all the world. You will wear it to-night next your heart, and as we dance together it will tell you how I love you."

But the girl frowned.

"I am afraid it will not go with my dress," she answered; "and, besides, the Chamberlain's nephew has sent me some real jewels, and everybody knows that jewels cost far more than flowers."

"Well, upon my word, you are very ungrateful," said the Student angrily; and he threw the rose into the street, where it fell into the gutter, and a cart-wheel went over it.

"Ungrateful!" said the girl. "I tell you what, you are very rude; and, after all, who are you? Only a Student. Why, I don't believe you have even got silver buckles to your shoes as the Chamberlain's nephew has"; and she got up from her chair and went into the house.

"What a silly thing Love is," said the Student as he walked away. "It is not half as useful as Logic, for it does not prove anything, and it is always telling one of things that are not going to happen, and making one believe things that are not true. In fact, it is quite unpractical, and, as in this age to be practical is everything, I shall go back to Philosophy and study Metaphysics."

So he returned to his room and pulled out a great dusty book, and began to read.

自私的巨人

~❧ The Selfish Giant ❧~

每天放學後，孩子們總會跑到巨人的花園裡玩耍。花園又大又美，還有柔軟的青草地。草地上到處點綴著美麗花卉，猶如星羅棋布，還有十二株桃樹，春天裡會綻放粉紅色與珍珠白色的柔美花朵，到了秋天便果實纍纍。鳥兒棲在枝頭引吭高歌，美妙的啼聲總會讓孩子們停止遊戲豎耳傾聽。「在這裡好開心喔！」大夥兒互相叫嚷著。

有一天，巨人回來了。之前他去康瓦爾找食人魔朋友，在那兒待了七年。七年過後，會話能力有限的他，要說的話都說完了，便決定回自家城堡。抵達時，他看見了孩子在花園玩耍。

「你們在這裡做什麼？」他用非常粗啞的聲音咆哮道，孩子們紛紛跑開。

「我的花園就是我的花園，」巨人說：「這點誰都能明白，除了我，誰也不許在這裡玩。」於是他築了一道高高的圍牆，並豎起一塊告示牌：

擅入者嚴懲不貸

這個巨人自私至極。

這一來，可憐的孩子們無處玩耍，他們雖然試著在路

E very afternoon, as they were coming from school, the children used to go and play in the Giant's garden.

It was a large lovely garden, with soft green grass. Here and there over the grass stood beautiful flowers like stars, and there were twelve peach-trees that in the spring-time broke out into delicate blossoms of pink and pearl, and in the autumn bore rich fruit. The birds sat on the trees and sang so sweetly that the children used to stop their games in order to listen to them. "How happy we are here!" they cried to each other.

One day the Giant came back. He had been to visit his friend the Cornish ogre, and had stayed with him for seven years. After the seven years were over he had said all that he had to say, for his conversation was limited, and he determined to return to his own castle. When he arrived he saw the children playing in the garden.

"What are you doing here?" he cried in a very gruff voice, and the children ran away.

"My own garden is my own garden," said the Giant; "any one can understand that, and I will allow nobody to play in it but myself." So he built a high wall all round it, and put up a notice-board.

TRESPASSERS
WILL BE
PROSECUTED

He was a very selfish Giant.

The poor children had now nowhere to play. They tried to play

上玩耍，但路上塵土瀰漫，到處都是硬石頭，他們不喜歡。他們常常在下課後，繞著高牆溜達，談論裡面的美麗花園。「以前在裡面玩的時候多開心哪！」他們說。

不久春天來臨，鄉間四處可見小花與小鳥。只有在自私巨人的花園裡還是冬天。鳥兒不想在裡面鳴唱，因為那裡沒有小孩，樹也忘了開花。曾有一朵美麗的花從草叢間冒出頭來，但一看到告示牌，不禁為孩子們感到難過，便溜回地底下繼續蟄伏。這時只有霜雪感到高興。「春天把這座園子遺忘了。」霜雪大喊道：「我們可以整年都待在這裡。」雪用大大的白色斗篷披覆草地，寒霜將所有樹木漆成銀白色。接著他們邀請北風前來同住，北風便來了。他裹著毛皮大衣，鎮日在花園裡四下呼嘯，把煙囪管帽都吹掀了。「這地方真叫人喜愛。」他說：「我們得邀冰雹來玩玩。」於是冰雹來了。他每天總要在城堡屋頂上劈哩啪啦砸上三個小時，直到把大部分瓦片都砸壞，又開始以最快的速度繞著花園一圈又一圈地飛奔。他身穿灰衣，吐氣如冰。

「我不明白，春天為什麼來得這麼晚？」自私的巨人坐在窗邊，看著寒冷雪白的花園說：「但願天氣趕快轉暖。」

誰知春天遲遲不來，夏天也一樣。秋天賜予每座花園金黃果實，巨人的花園裡卻什麼也沒有。「他太自私

on the road, but the road was very dusty and full of hard stones, and they did not like it. They used to wander round the high wall when their lessons were over, and talk about the beautiful garden inside. "How happy we were there," they said to each other.

Then the Spring came, and all over the country there were little blossoms and little birds. Only in the garden of the Selfish Giant it was still winter. The birds did not care to sing in it as there were no children, and the trees forgot to blossom. Once a beautiful flower put its head out from the grass, but when it saw the notice-board it was so sorry for the children that it slipped back into the ground again, and went off to sleep. The only people who were pleased were the Snow and the Frost. "Spring has forgotten this garden," they cried, "so we will live here all the year round." The Snow covered up the grass with her great white cloak, and the Frost painted all the trees silver. Then they invited the North Wind to stay with them, and he came. He was wrapped in furs, and he roared all day about the garden, and blew the chimney-pots down. "This is a delightful spot," he said, "we must ask the Hail on a visit." So the Hail came. Every day for three hours he rattled on the roof of the castle till he broke most of the slates, and then he ran round and round the garden as fast as he could go. He was dressed in grey, and his breath was like ice.

"I cannot understand why the Spring is so late in coming," said the Selfish Giant, as he sat at the window and looked out at his cold white garden; "I hope there will be a change in the weather."

But the Spring never came, nor the Summer. The Autumn gave golden fruit to every garden, but to the Giant's garden she gave none.

了。」秋天說。所以巨人的花園裡始終是冬天，北風、冰雹、和霜雪不停在樹枝間舞動。

有一天早晨，巨人醒著躺在床上，忽然聽見美妙的樂音。實在太悅耳了，他心想必定是國王的樂隊打這兒經過。其實只是一隻小紅雀在窗外啼叫，但他實在太久沒有在花園裡聽過鳥鳴，如今聽來竟成了世上最美的音樂。這時候，冰雹不再在他頭上舞動，北風也停止呼號，一陣宜人的香氣從敞開的窗口飄入。「我想春天終於來了。」巨人說著跳下床望向窗外。

他看見了什麼？

他看見了無與倫比的美好景象。孩子們從牆上一個小洞爬進來，此時坐在枝頭上。他看見每棵樹上都有一個小孩。樹木見到孩子們回來，開心得整株花朵盛開，還在孩子們的頭上輕搖臂膀。鳥兒飛來飛去，愉快地唧啾鳴囀，花兒透過青草仰天大笑。一片欣然的景象，卻獨有一個角落依然還是冬天。那是花園最遠的角落，有個小男孩站在那裡，由於個頭太小，攀不上樹枝，只能繞著樹晃來晃去，哭得十分傷心。那棵可憐的樹上仍覆著霜雪，北風也仍在樹梢呼嘯。「孩子，爬上來呀！」樹盡可能地彎低枝

"He is too selfish," she said. So it was always Winter there, and the North Wind, and the Hail, and the Frost, and the Snow danced about through the trees.

One morning the Giant was lying awake in bed when he heard some lovely music. It sounded so sweet to his ears that he thought it must be the King's musicians passing by. It was really only a little linnet singing outside his window, but it was so long since he had heard a bird sing in his garden that it seemed to him to be the most beautiful music in the world. Then the Hail stopped dancing over his head, and the North Wind ceased roaring, and a delicious perfume came to him through the open casement. "I believe the Spring has come at last," said the Giant; and he jumped out of bed and looked out.

What did he see?

He saw a most wonderful sight. Through a little hole in the wall the children had crept in, and they were sitting in the branches of the trees. In every tree that he could see there was a little child. And the trees were so glad to have the children back again that they had covered themselves with blossoms, and were waving their arms gently above the children's heads. The birds were flying about and twittering with delight, and the flowers were looking up through the green grass and laughing. It was a lovely scene, only in one corner it was still winter. It was the farthest corner of the garden, and in it was standing a little boy. He was so small that he could not reach up to the branches of the tree, and he was wandering all round it, crying bitterly. The poor tree was still quite covered with frost and snow, and the North Wind was blowing and roaring above it. "Climb up! little boy," said the Tree,

枒，偏偏男孩就是太小，爬不上去。

巨人往外一看，心軟了。

「以前的我多自私啊！」他說：「現在我知道春天為什麼不肯來了。我要把那個可憐的小男孩放到樹梢上，還要把牆拆了，讓我的花園永遠永遠都是孩子們的遊樂園。」他對自己的所作所為真的非常懊悔。

因此他悄悄下樓，輕手輕腳地打開前門，走進花園。不料孩子們一看見他，全都嚇得跑開了，花園再次陷入寒冬。只有那個小男孩沒逃走，因為他眼中滿是淚水，沒看見巨人走近。巨人偷偷走到他身後，輕輕將他托起，放上樹枝。樹瞬間開出花來，鳥兒也飛來，棲上枝頭鳴唱，小男孩張開雙臂，摟住巨人的脖子，還親了他一下。其他孩子見巨人不再凶惡，便紛紛跑回來，春天也尾隨而至。「孩子們，從現在起，這裡就是你們的花園了。」巨人說完，拿起一把大斧頭劈倒圍牆。中午十二點，民眾上市集時，看見巨人正和孩子們在一座前所未見的美麗花園裡玩耍。

孩子們玩了一整天，到了傍晚才來和巨人道別。

「咦，你們那個小同伴呢？」他說：「就是我放到樹

and it bent its branches down as low as it could; but the boy was too tiny.

And the Giant's heart melted as he looked out. "How selfish I have been!" he said; "now I know why the Spring would not come here. I will put that poor little boy on the top of the tree, and then I will knock down the wall, and my garden shall be the children's playground for ever and ever." He was really very sorry for what he had done.

So he crept downstairs and opened the front door quite softly, and went out into the garden. But when the children saw him they were so frightened that they all ran away, and the garden became winter again. Only the little boy did not run, for his eyes were so full of tears that he did not see the Giant coming. And the Giant stole up behind him and took him gently in his hand, and put him up into the tree. And the tree broke at once into blossom, and the birds came and sang on it, and the little boy stretched out his two arms and flung them round the Giant's neck, and kissed him. And the other children, when they saw that the Giant was not wicked any longer, came running back, and with them came the Spring. "It is your garden now, little children," said the Giant, and he took a great axe and knocked down the wall. And when the people were going to market at twelve o'clock they found the Giant playing with the children in the most beautiful garden they had ever seen.

All day long they played, and in the evening they came to the Giant to bid him good-bye.

"But where is your little companion?" he said: "the boy I put into

上去的那個小男孩。」巨人最喜歡他，因為男孩親了他。

「不知道，」孩子們回答：「他已經走了。」

「你們得告訴他，叫他明天一定要來。」巨人說。可是孩子們說不知道他住在哪裡，以前也從沒見過他。巨人覺得好傷心。

每天下午放學後，孩子們都會來找巨人玩。然而巨人最喜愛的那個小男孩再也沒有出現過。巨人對所有的孩子都很親切，卻仍渴望見到自己第一個交的小朋友，也不時提起他。「我多想見到他呀！」巨人老是這麼說。

過了許多年，巨人變得老邁虛弱，再也無法玩耍，便坐在巨大的扶手椅上看著孩子們嬉戲，同時欣賞自己的花園，說道：「我有許多美麗的花朵，但孩子才是最美的花。」

某個冬日清晨，巨人更衣時望向窗外。如今他不討厭冬天了，因為他知道春天只是在冬眠，花兒只是在休養生息。

忽然間，他訝異地揉揉眼睛，看了又看。眼前景象太不可思議了。只見花園最遠處的角落裡，有一棵樹上開滿漂亮的白花，金黃的枝枒垂掛著銀色果實，而樹下站著他最喜愛的那個小男孩。

巨人欣喜萬分地奔下樓，進到花園。他急匆匆穿越草地，來到男孩身邊，就近一看，不禁憤怒地漲紅了臉，問道：「是誰竟敢傷害你？」原來孩子的掌心有兩個釘痕，

the tree." The Giant loved him the best because he had kissed him.

"We don't know," answered the children; "he has gone away."

"You must tell him to be sure and come here to-morrow," said the Giant. But the children said that they did not know where he lived, and had never seen him before; and the Giant felt very sad.

Every afternoon, when school was over, the children came and played with the Giant. But the little boy whom the Giant loved was never seen again. The Giant was very kind to all the children, yet he longed for his first little friend, and often spoke of him. "How I would like to see him!" he used to say.

Years went over, and the Giant grew very old and feeble. He could not play about any more, so he sat in a huge armchair, and watched the children at their games, and admired his garden. "I have many beautiful flowers," he said; "but the children are the most beautiful flowers of all."

One winter morning he looked out of his window as he was dressing. He did not hate the Winter now, for he knew that it was merely the Spring asleep, and that the flowers were resting.

Suddenly he rubbed his eyes in wonder, and looked and looked. It certainly was a marvellous sight. In the farthest corner of the garden was a tree quite covered with lovely white blossoms. Its branches were all golden, and silver fruit hung down from them, and underneath it stood the little boy he had loved.

Downstairs ran the Giant in great joy, and out into the garden. He hastened across the grass, and came near to the child. And when he came quite close his face grew red with anger, and he said, "Who hath

小腳上也有兩個釘痕。

「是誰竟敢傷害你？」巨人咆哮道：「告訴我，我立刻提我的巨劍去殺了他。」

「不！」孩子回答：「這其實是愛的傷痕。」

「你是誰？」巨人才問完，心中忽然興起怪異的敬畏之情，在小孩面前跪了下來。

孩子對著巨人露出微笑說道：「你曾經讓我在你的花園裡玩，今天你就隨我到我的花園去吧，那裡是天堂。」

當天下午，孩子們跑進花園，發現巨人已倒在樹下死去，全身覆滿白花。

dared to wound thee?" For on the palms of the child's hands were the prints of two nails, and the prints of two nails were on the little feet.

"Who hath dared to wound thee?" cried the Giant; "tell me, that I may take my big sword and slay him."

"Nay!" answered the child; "but these are the wounds of Love."

"Who art thou?" said the Giant, and a strange awe fell on him, and he knelt before the little child.

And the child smiled on the Giant, and said to him, "You let me play once in your garden, to-day you shall come with me to my garden, which is Paradise."

And when the children ran in that afternoon, they found the Giant lying dead under the tree, all covered with white blossoms.

忠實的朋友

───◈───

The Devoted Friend

天早晨，老水鼠從洞裡探出頭來。他一雙眼睛又圓又亮，硬挺的灰鬚，尾巴有如一條長長的黑色彈性橡皮。小鴨子在池塘裡游來游去，簡直有如一群黃絲雀，而全身純白、一雙大紅腳的母鴨，正設法教他們如何在水中倒立。

　　「你們要是不學會倒立，就永遠進不了上流社會。」她一再地對孩子們說，並不時示範給他們看。但小鴨子不予理會，他們還太小，根本不知道進入上流社會有什麼好處。

　　「真是一群不聽話的孩子，」老水鼠嚷嚷道：「真該讓他們淹死算了。」

　　「話不能這麼說，」母鴨回答：「誰沒有個起步的時候？當父母的愈有耐心愈好。」

　　「哈！我完全不懂當父母的感覺。」水鼠說：「我不是個愛家的人，說實話，我從來沒結過婚，也從來不想結婚。愛情當然有它的優點，但友情更可貴。說真的，我不知道這世上還有什麼比忠實的友情更高貴或更難得的東西。」

　　「那麼請問一下，你認為忠實的朋友該盡哪些義務呢？」一隻綠雀開口問道，他就棲在一旁的柳樹上，無意間聽見他們的對話。

　　「是啊，這也正是我想知道的。」母鴨說著，往池塘的另一頭游去，以便好好地為孩子示範水中倒立。

One morning the old Water-rat put his head out of his hole. He had bright beady eyes and stiff grey whiskers and his tail was like a long bit of black india-rubber. The little ducks were swimming about in the pond, looking just like a lot of yellow canaries, and their mother, who was pure white with real red legs, was trying to teach them how to stand on their heads in the water.

"You will never be in the best society unless you can stand on your heads," she kept saying to them; and every now and then she showed them how it was done. But the little ducks paid no attention to her. They were so young that they did not know what an advantage it is to be in society at all.

"What disobedient children!" cried the old Water-rat; "they really deserve to be drowned."

"Nothing of the kind," answered the Duck, "every one must make a beginning, and parents cannot be too patient."

"Ah! I know nothing about the feelings of parents," said the Water-rat; "I am not a family man. In fact, I have never been married, and I never intend to be. Love is all very well in its way, but friendship is much higher. Indeed, I know of nothing in the world that is either nobler or rarer than a devoted friendship."

"And what, pray, is your idea of the duties of a devoted friend?" asked a Green Linnet, who was sitting in a willow-tree hard by, and had overheard the conversation.

"Yes, that is just what I want to know," said the Duck; and she swam away to the end of the pond, and stood upon her head, in order to give her children a good example.

「多愚蠢的問題！」水鼠大聲說：「我當然是希望忠實的朋友能對我忠實啊。」

「那你會怎麼回報呢？」小鳥問道，他在一根銀枝上晃蕩了一下，拍拍小翅膀。

「我不明白你的意思。」水鼠回答。

「關於這個話題，我來跟你說個故事吧。」綠雀說。

「故事和我有關嗎？」水鼠問：「有關的話我就聽，我最喜歡虛構的故事了。」

「對你很合用。」綠雀回答後飛了下來，歇在堤岸上，開始說起忠實朋友的故事。

「很久很久以前，」綠雀說：「有個老實的小夥子名叫漢斯。」

「他非常出色嗎？」水鼠問。

「不，」綠雀回答：「我覺得他一點也不出色，只是有一副好心腸，還有一張滑稽但和氣的圓臉。他獨自住在一間小茅屋，每天在花園裡工作。整個鄉間就數他的花園最美麗。那裡種了美洲石竹、麝香石竹、薺菜和長舌著。還有大馬士革玫瑰、黃玫瑰、淡紫色番紅花，金色、紫色與白色紫羅蘭，還有夢幻草、草甸碎米薺、馬鬱蘭、野羅勒、櫻草、鳶尾花、黃水仙和康乃馨，都按著年月時序依次盛開，一種花謝了，便由另一種取代，因此隨時都有美景可賞，有香氣可聞。

「小漢斯交遊廣闊，但磨坊主人大修是最忠實的一個

"What a silly question!" cried the Water-rat. "I should expect my devoted friend to be devoted to me, of course."

"And what would you do in return?" said the little bird, swinging upon a silver spray, and flapping his tiny wings.

"I don't understand you," answered the Water-rat.

"Let me tell you a story on the subject," said the Linnet.

"Is the story about me?" asked the Water-rat. "If so, I will listen to it, for I am extremely fond of fiction."

"It is applicable to you," answered the Linnet; and he flew down, and alighting upon the bank, he told the story of The Devoted Friend.

"Once upon a time," said the Linnet, "there was an honest little fellow named Hans."

"Was he very distinguished?" asked the Water-rat.

"No," answered the Linnet, "I don't think he was distinguished at all, except for his kind heart, and his funny round good-humoured face. He lived in a tiny cottage all by himself, and every day he worked in his garden. In all the country-side there was no garden so lovely as his. Sweet-william grew there, and Gilly-flowers, and Shepherds'-purses, and Fair-maids of France. There were damask Roses, and yellow Roses, lilac Crocuses, and gold, purple Violets and white. Columbine and Ladysmock, Marjoram and Wild Basil, the Cowslip and the Flower-de-luce, the Daffodil and the Clove-Pink bloomed or blossomed in their proper order as the months went by, one flower taking another flower's place, so that there were always beautiful things to look at, and pleasant odours to smell.

"Little Hans had a great many friends, but the most devoted

朋友。這位富有的磨坊主人對小漢斯的確忠心耿耿，每次經過他的花園，磨坊主人總會探過牆頭摘一大朵報春花或是一把香草，要是碰上水果季，就會採摘李子和櫻桃裝滿口袋。

「『真正的朋友就要共享一切。』磨坊主人常常這麼說，小漢斯便點頭微笑，對於朋友如此高尚的想法而深感自豪。

「老實說，街坊鄰居偶爾會覺得奇怪，儘管富有的磨坊主人在磨坊裡貯藏了一百袋麵粉，還養了六頭乳牛和一大群毛茸茸的綿羊，卻從未給過小漢斯任何回報。不過漢斯從不為這些事情傷腦筋，磨坊主人常說真正的友誼要無私無我，聽著這些高談闊論是漢斯最大的樂趣。

「總之，小漢斯在花園裡努力地工作。春天、夏天、秋天，他都快樂無比，可是冬天一來，他沒有水果或花可以拿到市場上賣，飢寒交迫下，他痛苦萬分，往往也沒吃晚餐，只靠幾片乾梨和幾顆堅果來果腹便上床了。冬天裡他也十分寂寞，因為磨坊主人從不來找他。

「『只要還下著雪，我去找小漢斯也沒用。』磨坊主人常對妻子這麼說：『因為當人遭遇困難，就應該讓他獨處，不該上門打擾。至少這是我對友情的想法，相信我是對的。所以我要等春天來了以後再去找他，到時他可以給

friend of all was big Hugh the Miller. Indeed, so devoted was the rich Miller to little Hans, that he would never go by his garden without leaning over the wall and plucking a large nosegay, or a handful of sweet herbs, or filling his pockets with plums and cherries if it was the fruit season.

"'Real friends should have everything in common,' the Miller used to say, and little Hans nodded and smiled, and felt very proud of having a friend with such noble ideas.

"Sometimes, indeed, the neighbours thought it strange that the rich Miller never gave little Hans anything in return, though he had a hundred sacks of flour stored away in his mill, and six milch cows, and a large flock of woolly sheep; but Hans never troubled his head about these things, and nothing gave him greater pleasure than to listen to all the wonderful things the Miller used to say about the unselfishness of true friendship.

"So little Hans worked away in his garden. During the spring, the summer, and the autumn he was very happy, but when the winter came, and he had no fruit or flowers to bring to the market, he suffered a good deal from cold and hunger, and often had to go to bed without any supper but a few dried pears or some hard nuts. In the winter, also, he was extremely lonely, as the Miller never came to see him then.

"'There is no good in my going to see little Hans as long as the snow lasts,' the Miller used to say to his wife, 'for when people are in trouble they should be left alone, and not be bothered by visitors. That at least is my idea about friendship, and I am sure I am right. So I shall wait till the spring comes, and then I shall pay him a visit, and he will

我一大籃報春花，他會很開心。』

「『你確實很懂得體貼人。』妻子回答道，她坐在舒適的扶手椅上，一旁是燒著松木的熊熊爐火。『你真的很體貼。聽你談論友誼是一大樂事。我敢說就連牧師也無法說得這麼好，雖然他住在一棟三層樓房，小指還戴著金戒。』

「『可是我們不能邀小漢斯到家裡來嗎？』磨坊主人的小兒子說：『要是可憐的漢斯不好過，我就把一半的麥片粥分給他，也讓他看我養的白兔。』

「『你這個笨小子！』磨坊主人大吼：『真不知道送你去上學有什麼用，書都讀到哪去了？我說啊，要是小漢斯到家裡來，看見我們溫暖的爐火、豐盛的晚餐和大桶的紅酒，他可能會心生忌妒，而忌妒是最可怕的了，它會毀了人的本性。我絕對不能讓漢斯被毀。我是他最好的朋友，我會永遠守護他，不讓他受到任何誘惑。再說，如果漢斯來了，他可能會要我賒一點麵粉給他，這可不行。麵粉和友情是兩碼子事，不能混為一談。喏，這兩個詞寫法不同，意思也大不同，任誰都看得出來。』

「『你說得真是頭頭是道！』磨坊主人的妻子說，同時給自己倒了一大杯溫麥酒。『我覺得好睏，就好像上教堂似的。』

be able to give me a large basket of primroses and that will make him so happy.'

"'You are certainly very thoughtful about others,' answered the Wife, as she sat in her comfortable armchair by the big pinewood fire; 'very thoughtful indeed. It is quite a treat to hear you talk about friendship. I am sure the clergyman himself could not say such beautiful things as you do, though he does live in a three-storied house, and wear a gold ring on his little finger.'

"'But could we not ask little Hans up here?' said the Miller's youngest son. 'If poor Hans is in trouble I will give him half my porridge, and show him my white rabbits.'

"'What a silly boy you are!' cried the Miller; 'I really don't know what is the use of sending you to school. You seem not to learn anything. Why, if little Hans came up here, and saw our warm fire, and our good supper, and our great cask of red wine, he might get envious, and envy is a most terrible thing, and would spoil anybody's nature. I certainly will not allow Hans' nature to be spoiled. I am his best friend, and I will always watch over him, and see that he is not led into any temptations. Besides, if Hans came here, he might ask me to let him have some flour on credit, and that I could not do. Flour is one thing, and friendship is another, and they should not be confused. Why, the words are spelt differently, and mean quite different things. Everybody can see that.'

"'How well you talk!' said the Miller's Wife, pouring herself out a large glass of warm ale; 'really I feel quite drowsy. It is just like being in church.'

「『表現好的人很多，』磨坊主人回答說：『但能言善道的人少之又少，可見得言語比行困難得多，也細膩得多。』他一臉嚴肅地看著餐桌對面的小兒子，只見他羞愧萬分地低垂著頭，面紅耳赤地哭了起來，淚水滴進茶杯裡。但是他年紀實在太小，你得諒解。」

「故事說完了？」水鼠問道。

「當然還沒，這才剛開始呢。」綠雀回答。

「那你就落伍了，」水鼠說：「現今說故事的高手都是從結尾說起，然後再講開頭，最後才講中段。這是新方法。前幾天有個評論家和一位年輕人在池塘邊散步，我聽他說了好多。他滔滔不絕，想必說得沒錯，因為他戴了藍色眼鏡、頂著大光頭。年輕人每說一句，他就回一句『哼！』不過還是請你繼續說故事吧。我好喜歡那個磨坊主人，我自己也有各種高明的感想，所以和他很有共鳴。」

「好吧，」綠雀說著，一下用這隻腳蹦跳，一下換另一隻腳。「冬天一過，當報春花開始綻放淺黃色星形花瓣，磨坊主人便對妻子說他要去找小漢斯。

「『哎喲，你心腸太好了！』妻子高喊：『你老是想著別人。對了，別忘了帶大籃子去裝花。』

「於是磨坊主人用堅固鐵鍊把風車葉片綁起來，挽著

"'Lots of people act well,' answered the Miller; 'but very few people talk well, which shows that talking is much the more difficult thing of the two, and much the finer thing also'; and he looked sternly across the table at his little son, who felt so ashamed of himself that he hung his head down, and grew quite scarlet, and began to cry into his tea. However, he was so young that you must excuse him."

"Is that the end of the story?" asked the Water-rat.

"Certainly not," answered the Linnet, "that is the beginning."

"Then you are quite behind the age," said the Water-rat. "Every good story-teller nowadays starts with the end, and then goes on to the beginning, and concludes with the middle. That is the new method. I heard all about it the other day from a critic who was walking round the pond with a young man. He spoke of the matter at great length, and I am sure he must have been right, for he had blue spectacles and a bald head, and whenever the young man made any remark, he always answered 'Pooh!' But pray go on with your story. I like the Miller immensely. I have all kinds of beautiful sentiments myself, so there is a great sympathy between us."

"Well," said the Linnet, hopping now on one leg and now on the other, "as soon as the winter was over, and the primroses began to open their pale yellow stars, the Miller said to his wife that he would go down and see little Hans.

"'Why, what a good heart you have!' cried his Wife; 'you are always thinking of others. And mind you take the big basket with you for the flowers.'

"So the Miller tied the sails of the windmill together with a strong

籃子下山去了。

「『早啊，小漢斯。』磨坊主人說。

「『早。』漢斯倚著鐵鍬，笑得合不攏嘴。

「『這個冬天你過得如何？』磨坊主人問。

「『哎呀，』漢斯喊道：『非常感謝你的關心，你真是大好人。可惜我過得挺辛苦的，不過現在春天來了，我好開心，我的花兒都開得很好。』

「『冬天裡我們常常聊起你呢，漢斯。』磨坊主人說：『總想著不知你過得怎麼樣。』

「『你們人真好。』漢斯說：『我還有點擔心你們把我給忘了。』

「『漢斯，沒想到你會說這種話。』磨坊主人說：『友情是長存不忘的，這正是它美好的地方，不過你恐怕不懂生活的詩意吧。對了，你的報春花開得可真美！』

「『可不是嘛！』漢斯說：『最幸運的是花還開了這麼多。我要把花帶到市集去賣給市長的女兒，再用那筆錢買回我的獨輪推車。』

「『買回你的獨輪推車？你該不是說你把它賣了吧？這麼做未免太笨了！』

「『不瞞你說，』漢斯說：『我也是逼不得已。你知道冬天對我來說很難捱，我根本沒錢買麵包。所以我先賣了做禮拜時要穿的外套上的銀鈕扣，然後是銀鍊子，再賣

iron chain, and went down the hill with the basket on his arm.

"'Good morning, little Hans,' said the Miller.

"'Good morning,' said Hans, leaning on his spade, and smiling from ear to ear.

"'And how have you been all the winter?' said the Miller.

"'Well, really,' cried Hans, 'it is very good of you to ask, very good indeed. I am afraid I had rather a hard time of it, but now the spring has come, and I am quite happy, and all my flowers are doing well.'

"'We often talked of you during the winter, Hans,' said the Miller, 'and wondered how you were getting on.'

"'That was kind of you,' said Hans; 'I was half afraid you had forgotten me.'

"'Hans, I am surprised at you,' said the Miller; 'friendship never forgets. That is the wonderful thing about it, but I am afraid you don't understand the poetry of life. How lovely your primroses are looking, by-the-bye!"

"'They are certainly very lovely,' said Hans, 'and it is a most lucky thing for me that I have so many. I am going to bring them into the market and sell them to the Burgomaster's daughter, and buy back my wheelbarrow with the money.'

"'Buy back your wheelbarrow? You don't mean to say you have sold it? What a very stupid thing to do!'

"'Well, the fact is,' said Hans, 'that I was obliged to. You see the winter was a very bad time for me, and I really had no money at all to buy bread with. So I first sold the silver buttons off my Sunday coat, and then I sold my silver chain, and then I sold my big pipe, and at last

掉大菸斗，最後才賣掉獨輪推車。但我現在要把它們全買回來。』

「『漢斯，』磨坊主人說：『我的獨輪推車給你吧。它狀況不是太好，說實話，推車有一邊沒了，車輪輻條也有點問題，但無論如何，我還是把它送給你。我知道自己非常慷慨，很多人會覺得我愚蠢至極才把它送走，但我可不像其他人。我認為慷慨是友情的基本，何況我自己已經買了新推車。沒錯，你大可以放心，我會把我的推車給你。』

「『呵，你真是太慷慨了。』小漢斯說，滑稽的圓臉上喜形於色。『我很輕鬆就能把它修好，因為我家有一塊木板可以使用。』

「『木板！』磨坊主人說：『太好了，我正需要木板來修補穀倉屋頂。屋頂上破了個大洞，不堵上的話，穀物全都會受潮。你剛好提起這件事，實在太巧了！還挺不可思議的，果然好心總有好報。我把獨輪推車給了你，現在換你把木板給我。當然，推車比木板貴多了，但真摯的朋友絕不會在意這種事。請你馬上去拿木板，我今天就可以動手修葺穀倉。』

「『沒問題，』小漢斯大聲說，隨即跑進小屋拖出木板。

「『這塊木板不是很大，』磨坊主人看著木板說：『我補好穀倉屋頂後，只怕你就沒得修推車了，不過這當

I sold my wheelbarrow. But I am going to buy them all back again now.'

"'Hans,' said the Miller, 'I will give you my wheelbarrow. It is not in very good repair; indeed, one side is gone, and there is something wrong with the wheel-spokes; but in spite of that I will give it to you. I know it is very generous of me, and a great many people would think me extremely foolish for parting with it, but I am not like the rest of the world. I think that generosity is the essence of friendship, and, besides, I have got a new wheelbarrow for myself. Yes, you may set your mind at ease, I will give you my wheelbarrow.'

"'Well, really, that is generous of you,' said little Hans, and his funny round face glowed all over with pleasure. 'I can easily put it in repair, as I have a plank of wood in the house.'

"'A plank of wood!' said the Miller; 'why, that is just what I want for the roof of my barn. There is a very large hole in it, and the corn will all get damp if I don't stop it up. How lucky you mentioned it! It is quite remarkable how one good action always breeds another. I have given you my wheelbarrow, and now you are going to give me your plank. Of course, the wheelbarrow is worth far more than the plank, but true, friendship never notices things like that. Pray get it at once, and I will set to work at my barn this very day.'

"'Certainly,' cried little Hans, and he ran into the shed and dragged the plank out.

"'It is not a very big plank,' said the Miller, looking at it, 'and I am afraid that after I have mended my barn-roof there won't be any left for you to mend the wheelbarrow with; but, of course, that is not my

然怪不得我。好啦，我既然送了你獨輪推車，你想必很樂意送我一些花做為回報吧。籃子在這兒，注意要裝滿一點。』

「『滿一點？』小漢斯憂心忡忡地問，因為那只籃子不是普通的大，他知道要是裝滿一籃，就再沒有花可以帶到市集去賣，他實在急著想買回銀鈕扣。

「『我說真的，』磨坊主人回應道：『我都把推車送你了，只是跟你討幾朵花不算過分吧。或許是我錯了，但我原以為友情，真正的友情，應該是毫無一點私心。』

「『我親愛的朋友啊，我的摯友啊，』小漢斯高喊：『花園裡的花歡迎你全部拿走。無論何時，我都寧可把銀鈕扣擺一邊，聽取你的忠告。』話畢，他便跑去摘下所有美麗的報春花，裝滿磨坊主人的籃子。

「『再見了，小漢斯，』磨坊主人說著扛起木板、提起大籃子，爬上山去。

「『再見。』小漢斯說。接著他歡天喜地地挖起土來，想到獨輪推車就開心得不得了。

「第二天，他正在門廊上釘掛忍冬，忽然聽見磨坊主人從大路上呼喊他。他連忙跳下梯子，跑過花園，越過牆頭往外看。

「只見磨坊主人揹著一大袋麵粉。

「『親愛的小漢斯，』磨坊主人說：『你願意幫我扛這袋麵粉去市集嗎？』

fault. And now, as I have given you my wheelbarrow, I am sure you would like to give me some flowers in return. Here is the basket, and mind you fill it quite full.'

"'Quite full?' said little Hans, rather sorrowfully, for it was really a very big basket, and he knew that if he filled it he would have no flowers left for the market and he was very anxious to get his silver buttons back.

"'Well, really,' answered the Miller, 'as I have given you my wheelbarrow, I don't think that it is much to ask you for a few flowers. I may be wrong, but I should have thought that friendship, true friendship, was quite free from selfishness of any kind.'

"'My dear friend, my best friend,' cried little Hans, 'you are welcome to all the flowers in my garden. I would much sooner have your good opinion than my silver buttons, any day'; and he ran and plucked all his pretty primroses, and filled the Miller's basket.

"'Good-bye, little Hans,' said the Miller, as he went up the hill with the plank on his shoulder, and the big basket in his hand.

"'Good-bye,' said little Hans, and he began to dig away quite merrily, he was so pleased about the wheelbarrow.

"The next day he was nailing up some honeysuckle against the porch, when he heard the Miller's voice calling to him from the road. So he jumped off the ladder, and ran down the garden, and looked over the wall.

"There was the Miller with a large sack of flour on his back.

"'Dear little Hans,' said the Miller, 'would you mind carrying this sack of flour for me to market?'

「『實在抱歉，』漢斯說：『但我今天真的很忙。有好多藤蔓要釘掛，好多花要澆水，還有一大片草地要滾壓。』

「『哦，是嘛？』磨坊主人說：『我覺得我都要送你推車了，你要是拒絕，未免太不講道義。』

「『千萬別這麼說，』小漢斯喊道：『我絕對不會不講道義。』他跑進屋裡拿了帽子，便扛起大大的麵粉袋，拖著沉重的腳步往前走。

「那天天氣炎熱，路上塵土漫天，漢斯還走不到六里路，就累得不得不坐下休息。然而他仍然鼓起勇氣繼續前進，最後終於到達市集。他在那裡等了一段時間，用極好的價錢賣掉麵粉之後，立刻趕回家，因為他擔心要是逗留得太晚，途中可能會遇上強盜。

「『真是辛苦的一天，』小漢斯上床就寢時對自己說：『但幸好沒有拒絕磨坊主人，他畢竟是我最好的朋友，再說他還要送我獨輪推車。』

「次日一早，磨坊主人來收麵粉的錢，不料小漢斯前一天太過疲憊，還沒起床。

「『真沒想到，』磨坊主人說：『你竟然這麼懶。說真的，我都要把推車送你了，我還以為你可能會勤快一點。懶惰是一大罪惡，我可不想交個懶惰或遊手好閒的朋友。你別怪我有話直說，要不是拿你當朋友，我當然不會這麼做。但如果不能有什麼說什麼，友情還有什麼用？討

"'Oh, I am so sorry,' said Hans, 'but I am really very busy to-day. I have got all my creepers to nail up, and all my flowers to water, and all my grass to roll.'

"'Well, really,' said the Miller, 'I think that, considering that I am going to give you my wheelbarrow, it is rather unfriendly of you to refuse.'

"'Oh, don't say that,' cried little Hans, 'I wouldn't be unfriendly for the whole world'; and he ran in for his cap, and trudged off with the big sack on his shoulders.

"It was a very hot day, and the road was terribly dusty, and before Hans had reached the sixth milestone he was so tired that he had to sit down and rest. However, he went on bravely, and as last he reached the market. After he had waited there some time, he sold the sack of flour for a very good price, and then he returned home at once, for he was afraid that if he stopped too late he might meet some robbers on the way.

"'It has certainly been a hard day,' said little Hans to himself as he was going to bed, 'but I am glad I did not refuse the Miller, for he is my best friend, and, besides, he is going to give me his wheelbarrow.'

"Early the next morning the Miller came down to get the money for his sack of flour, but little Hans was so tired that he was still in bed.

"'Upon my word,' said the Miller, 'you are very lazy. Really, considering that I am going to give you my wheelbarrow, I think you might work harder. Idleness is a great sin, and I certainly don't like any of my friends to be idle or sluggish. You must not mind my speaking quite plainly to you. Of course I should not dream of doing so if I were

好諂媚的好聽話誰都會說，可是忠言逆耳，真正的朋友不會在乎傷你的心。老實說，真正的莫逆之交會寧可傷你的心，因為他知道這樣才是為你好。』

「『真的很抱歉，』小漢斯揉著眼睛脫下睡帽說：『但我太累了，所以想多躺一會兒，聽聽鳥鳴。你知道嗎？每當聽了鳥鳴，我總會更有幹勁。』

「『那正好，』磨坊主人拍拍小漢斯的背說：『因為我希望你趕快換好衣服，上山到磨坊來幫我修補穀倉屋頂。』

「可憐的小漢斯急著想到自己的花園幹活，因為他已經兩天沒澆花了，可是他又不想拒絕磨坊主人，他們畢竟是那麼要好的朋友。

「『我要是說沒空，你會不會覺得我不講道義？』他用害羞膽怯的聲音問道。

「『我說真的，』磨坊主人說：『你想想，我都準備要把獨輪推車送你了，這點要求不過分吧。不過當然了，你要是不肯來，我也只好自己做了。』

「『不，萬萬不可！』小漢斯高喊，他跳下床換好衣服，前往穀倉。

「『他在那兒忙了一整天，直到太陽下山，日落時磨坊主人來查看進展。

「『你把屋頂的洞補好了嗎，小漢斯？』磨坊主人愉快地高喊。

not your friend. But what is the good of friendship if one cannot say exactly what one means? Anybody can say charming things and try to please and to flatter, but a true friend always says unpleasant things, and does not mind giving pain. Indeed, if he is a really true friend he prefers it, for he knows that then he is doing good.'

"'I am very sorry,' said little Hans, rubbing his eyes and pulling off his night-cap, 'but I was so tired that I thought I would lie in bed for a little time, and listen to the birds singing. Do you know that I always work better after hearing the birds sing?'

"'Well, I am glad of that,' said the Miller, clapping little Hans on the back, 'for I want you to come up to the mill as soon as you are dressed, and mend my barn-roof for me.'

"Poor little Hans was very anxious to go and work in his garden, for his flowers had not been watered for two days, but he did not like to refuse the Miller, as he was such a good friend to him.

"'Do you think it would be unfriendly of me if I said I was busy?' he inquired in a shy and timid voice.

"'Well, really,' answered the Miller, 'I do not think it is much to ask of you, considering that I am going to give you my wheelbarrow; but of course if you refuse I will go and do it myself.'

"'Oh! on no account,' cried little Hans and he jumped out of bed, and dressed himself, and went up to the barn.

"He worked there all day long, till sunset, and at sunset the Miller came to see how he was getting on.

"'Have you mended the hole in the roof yet, little Hans?' cried the Miller in a cheery voice.

「『都補好了。』小漢斯一面回答，一面爬下樓梯。

「『呵！』磨坊主人說：『人生最大的樂事莫過於為他人付出。』

「『聽你說話真是天大的殊榮，』小漢斯回答，同時抹抹額頭上的汗坐下來：『是至高無上的殊榮。但我恐怕永遠不會有這麼高明的觀點。』

「『你終究會有的，』磨坊主人說：『只是你得更努力。目前你只是在實踐友誼，總有一天你也會懂得理論。』

「『你真的這麼想？』小漢斯問。

「『毫無疑問，』磨坊主人回答：『但既然你已修好屋頂，還是趕快回家休息，因為明天我想要你替我到山裡放羊。』

「可憐的小漢斯聽了一聲也不敢吭。隔天一大清早，磨坊主人趕著羊群來到小屋，漢斯便帶著羊出發上山去。他來回就耗了一整天，回到家後精疲力竭，坐在椅子上就睡著了，直到天大亮才醒來。

「『今天能在花園裡幹活了，多愜意啊！』他說著立刻忙和起來。

「但不知怎地，他就是沒法好好照顧他的花，他的朋友磨坊主人老是跑來找他，一下要他花很長的時間跑腿辦差，一下叫他到磨坊裡幫忙。小漢斯有時苦惱不已，唯恐花兒會以為自己被他遺忘了，但他心想著磨坊主人是他最

"'It is quite mended,' answered little Hans, coming down the ladder.

"'Ah!' said the Miller, 'there is no work so delightful as the work one does for others.'

"'It is certainly a great privilege to hear you talk,' answered little Hans, sitting down, and wiping his forehead, 'a very great privilege. But I am afraid I shall never have such beautiful ideas as you have.'

"'Oh! they will come to you,' said the Miller, 'but you must take more pains. At present you have only the practice of friendship; some day you will have the theory also.'

"'Do you really think I shall?' asked little Hans.

"'I have no doubt of it,' answered the Miller, 'but now that you have mended the roof, you had better go home and rest, for I want you to drive my sheep to the mountain to-morrow.'

"Poor little Hans was afraid to say anything to this, and early the next morning the Miller brought his sheep round to the cottage, and Hans started off with them to the mountain. It took him the whole day to get there and back; and when he returned he was so tired that he went off to sleep in his chair, and did not wake up till it was broad daylight.

"'What a delightful time I shall have in my garden,' he said, and he went to work at once.

"But somehow he was never able to look after his flowers at all, for his friend the Miller was always coming round and sending him off on long errands, or getting him to help at the mill. Little Hans was very much distressed at times, as he was afraid his flowers would think

好的朋友，藉此自我安慰。『再說，』他老是這麼說：『他要把他的獨輪推車送我，這可是再慷慨不過的舉動了。』

「於是小漢斯賣力地為磨坊主人做事，磨坊主人則講述各種關於友情的美好特點，漢斯會把他的話記在筆記本上，晚上不時拿出來複習，因為他非常勤奮好學。

「有一天晚上，小漢斯坐在火爐邊，門忽然咚咚大響。那天晚上風狂雨急，風在屋子四周淒厲呼嘯，因此他起初以為只是風雨聲。不料又響起第二陣敲門聲，緊接著第三次，聲音比前兩次都響亮。

「『應該是哪個可憐的旅人。』小漢斯對自己說，便跑去開門。

「只見門口站著磨坊主人，他一手提著燈籠，另一手拿著一根粗柺杖。

「『親愛的小漢斯，』磨坊主人大喊：『我遇上大麻煩了。我的小兒子跌下樓梯摔傷了，我得去找大夫。可是他住得好遠，今晚風雨又這麼大，我忽然想到，最好還是你能幫我跑一趟。你也知道，我要把推車送你，為了公平起見，你總應該有所回報吧。』

「『那是當然，』小漢斯喊道：『你來找我可以說是我的榮幸，我馬上出發。不過你的燈籠得借我用用，天色這麼黑，我怕會跌進山溝。』

he had forgotten them, but he consoled himself by the reflection that the Miller was his best friend. 'Besides,' he used to say, 'he is going to give me his wheelbarrow, and that is an act of pure generosity.'

"So little Hans worked away for the Miller, and the Miller said all kinds of beautiful things about friendship, which Hans took down in a note-book, and used to read over at night, for he was a very good scholar.

"Now it happened that one evening little Hans was sitting by his fireside when a loud rap came at the door. It was a very wild night, and the wind was blowing and roaring round the house so terribly that at first he thought it was merely the storm. But a second rap came, and then a third, louder than any of the others.

"'It is some poor traveller,' said little Hans to himself, and he ran to the door.

"There stood the Miller with a lantern in one hand and a big stick in the other.

"'Dear little Hans,' cried the Miller, 'I am in great trouble. My little boy has fallen off a ladder and hurt himself, and I am going for the Doctor. But he lives so far away, and it is such a bad night, that it has just occurred to me that it would be much better if you went instead of me. You know I am going to give you my wheelbarrow, and so, it is only fair that you should do something for me in return.'

"'Certainly,' cried little Hans, 'I take it quite as a compliment your coming to me, and I will start off at once. But you must lend me your lantern, as the night is so dark that I am afraid I might fall into the ditch.'

「『真對不住，』磨坊主人回答：『但這是我新買的燈籠，萬一弄壞了，損失可不小。』

「『那沒關係，我不提燈籠也行。』小漢斯喊道，接著他取下毛皮大衣與保暖的大紅帽，繫上圍巾便出發。

「好可怕的暴風雨！夜色黑漆漆，小漢斯幾乎什麼也看不見，甚至被大風吹得站都站不穩。然而他勇往直前，走了約莫三小時後，終於來到醫生家，他敲了門。

「『誰呀？』醫生喊道，同時從臥室窗口探頭出來。

「『是我，小漢斯，大夫。』

「『有什麼事嗎，小漢斯？』

「『磨坊主人的兒子從樓梯摔下來，受了傷，磨坊主人想請你馬上去一趟。』

「『好吧！』醫生隨即命人備好馬、他的大靴子和燈籠，下樓後騎上馬，便往磨坊主人家去，小漢斯跟在後頭費力跋涉。

「誰知風雨愈來愈猛烈，大雨如注，小漢斯看不清前路，也跟不上馬的速度，最後終於走岔了路，迷失在荒原上。那裡十分危險，到處都是深深的坑洞，可憐的小漢斯就這麼淹死了。第二天，幾個牧羊人發現他漂浮在一大片水面上，便將他的遺體搬回小屋。

"'I am very sorry,' answered the Miller, 'but it is my new lantern, and it would be a great loss to me if anything happened to it.'

"'Well, never mind, I will do without it,' cried little Hans, and he took down his great fur coat, and his warm scarlet cap, and tied a muffler round his throat, and started off.

"What a dreadful storm it was! The night was so black that little Hans could hardly see, and the wind was so strong that he could scarcely stand. However, he was very courageous, and after he had been walking about three hours, he arrived at the Doctor's house, and knocked at the door.

"'Who is there?' cried the Doctor, putting his head out of his bedroom window.

"'Little Hans, Doctor.'

"'What do you want, little Hans?'

"'The Miller's son has fallen from a ladder, and has hurt himself, and the Miller wants you to come at once.'

"'All right!' said the Doctor; and he ordered his horse, and his big boots, and his lantern, and came downstairs, and rode off in the direction of the Miller's house, little Hans trudging behind him.

"But the storm grew worse and worse, and the rain fell in torrents, and little Hans could not see where he was going, or keep up with the horse. At last he lost his way, and wandered off on the moor, which was a very dangerous place, as it was full of deep holes, and there poor little Hans was drowned. His body was found the next day by some goatherds, floating in a great pool of water, and was brought back by them to the cottage.

「所有人都去參加小漢斯的葬禮，因為他人緣奇佳，磨坊主人擔任主祭。

「『我是他最好的朋友，』磨坊主人說：『主位應該給我才公平。』因此他穿著黑色長斗篷走在隊伍最前面，不時用一條大手帕抹抹眼睛。

「『小漢斯一死，對每個人都是一大損失。』鐵匠說道。這時葬禮已結束，大夥兒都舒舒服服坐在小旅店裡，喝著香料酒、吃著甜蛋糕。

「『總之對我是一大損失。』磨坊主人答腔：『唉，我等於是已經把獨輪推車送他了，這下子我還真不知該拿推車怎麼辦。放在家裡占位子，賣又賣不了幾個錢，因為實在太破了。以後我一定不要再送東西給人。人太慷慨果然是自找麻煩。』」

「然後呢？」停了大半晌後，水鼠問道。

「故事說完啦。」綠雀說。

「那磨坊主人後來怎麼樣了？」水鼠問。

「噢！我真不知道，而且我根本不在乎。」綠雀回答。

「可見得你天生就沒有同情心。」水鼠說。

「你好像沒聽懂故事的寓意。」綠雀說道。

「故事的什麼？」水鼠尖叫道。

「寓意。」

"Everybody went to little Hans' funeral, as he was so popular, and the Miller was the chief mourner.

"'As I was his best friend,' said the Miller, 'it is only fair that I should have the best place'; so he walked at the head of the procession in a long black cloak, and every now and then he wiped his eyes with a big pocket-handkerchief.

"'Little Hans is certainly a great loss to every one,' said the Blacksmith, when the funeral was over, and they were all seated comfortably in the inn, drinking spiced wine and eating sweet cakes.

"'A great loss to me at any rate,' answered the Miller; 'why, I had as good as given him my wheelbarrow, and now I really don't know what to do with it. It is very much in my way at home, and it is in such bad repair that I could not get anything for it if I sold it. I will certainly take care not to give away anything again. One always suffers for being generous.'"

"Well?" said the Water-rat, after a long pause.

"Well, that is the end," said the Linnet.

"But what became of the Miller?" asked the Water-rat.

"Oh! I really don't know," replied the Linnet; "and I am sure that I don't care."

"It is quite evident then that you have no sympathy in your nature," said the Water-rat.

"I am afraid you don't quite see the moral of the story," remarked the Linnet.

"The what?" screamed the Water-rat.

"The moral."

「你是說這個故事有寓意？」

「當然。」綠雀說。

「真是的，」水鼠氣呼呼地說：「你開始說故事以前就應該告訴我呀。你要是先說了，我絕對不會聽，事實上我應該像那個評論家一樣『啐』一聲。不過現在也不遲。」於是他扯開喉嚨，用力「啐」了一聲，尾巴一掃就回洞裡去了。

「你覺得水鼠怎麼樣？」幾分鐘後，母鴨划上前來問道。「他有很多優點，但我個人難免會站在母親的立場，只要看到打算一輩子打光棍的單身漢就會淚水盈眶。」

「我只怕是惹惱他了。」綠雀回答：「因為我跟他說了一個有寓意的故事。」

「哎呀！這向來是很危險的事。」母鴨說。

我舉雙手贊同。

"Do you mean to say that the story has a moral?"

"Certainly," said the Linnet.

"Well, really," said the Water-rat, in a very angry manner, "I think you should have told me that before you began. If you had done so, I certainly would not have listened to you; in fact, I should have said 'Pooh,' like the critic. However, I can say it now"; so he shouted out "Pooh" at the top of his voice, gave a whisk with his tail, and went back into his hole.

"And how do you like the Water-rat?" asked the Duck, who came paddling up some minutes afterwards. "He has a great many good points, but for my own part I have a mother's feelings, and I can never look at a confirmed bachelor without the tears coming into my eyes."

"I am rather afraid that I have annoyed him," answered the Linnet. "The fact is, that I told him a story with a moral."

"Ah! that is always a very dangerous thing to do," said the Duck.

And I quite agree with her.

了不起的火箭炮

The Remarkable Rocket

國王的兒子結婚在即，舉國歡騰。他已經等候新娘一整年，如今她終於到達了。新娘是俄國公主，千里迢迢從芬蘭坐著六匹馴鹿拉的雪橇前來。雪橇的造型像一隻巨大的金色天鵝，小公主就坐在天鵝的翅膀之間。她的貂皮長袍長達腳邊，頭上戴著一頂銀色薄紗小帽，膚色白得有如她長年居住的雪宮。她是那樣地白皙，當雪橇駛過街道，民眾無不驚嘆。「她就像白玫瑰呀！」眾人高呼，並從陽台上朝她撒下花朵。

王子正在城堡門口等著迎接她。他有一對迷濛的紫羅蘭色眼睛，頭髮猶如純金。一見到公主，他立刻單膝下跪親吻她的手。

「你的畫像很美，」他低聲說道：「但你比畫像還要美。」小公主不禁羞紅了臉。

「她本來像白玫瑰，」一名年輕侍從對身旁的同伴說：「現在卻像紅玫瑰了。」宮中上下都十分歡喜。

接下來三天，人人一開口就是：「白玫瑰，紅玫瑰，紅玫瑰，白玫瑰。」國王於是下令為那名侍從加薪一倍。由於他根本沒有薪俸，加薪也沒什麼用，但這被當成了莫大殊榮，照例要刊登在宮廷公報上。

三天後舉行婚禮，儀式盛大隆重，新郎和新娘攜手走

The King's son was going to be married, so there were general rejoicings. He had waited a whole year for his bride, and at last she had arrived. She was a Russian Princess, and had driven all the way from Finland in a sledge drawn by six reindeer. The sledge was shaped like a great golden swan, and between the swan's wings lay the little Princess herself. Her long ermine-cloak reached right down to her feet, on her head was a tiny cap of silver tissue, and she was as pale as the Snow Palace in which she had always lived. So pale was she that as she drove through the streets all the people wondered. "She is like a white rose!" they cried, and they threw down flowers on her from the balconies.

At the gate of the Castle the Prince was waiting to receive her. He had dreamy violet eyes, and his hair was like fine gold. When he saw her he sank upon one knee, and kissed her hand.

"Your picture was beautiful," he murmured, "but you are more beautiful than your picture"; and the little Princess blushed.

"She was like a white rose before," said a young Page to his neighbour, "but she is like a red rose now"; and the whole Court was delighted.

For the next three days everybody went about saying, "White rose, Red rose, Red rose, White rose"; and the King gave orders that the Page's salary was to be doubled. As he received no salary at all this was not of much use to him, but it was considered a great honour, and was duly published in the Court Gazette.

When the three days were over the marriage was celebrated. It was a magnificent ceremony, and the bride and bridegroom walked

在綴著小珍珠的紫色絲絨華蓋下。接下來是長達五個小時的國宴，王子與公主坐在大廳最上位，用剔透的水晶杯喝酒。只有真心相愛的戀人才能用這種杯子飲酒，若是被不忠的嘴唇碰到，杯子就會變得混濁而暗淡無光。

「一眼就能看出他們是相愛的，」小侍從說：「正如水晶一眼就能看透！」國王又再次為他加薪。

「多光榮啊！」大臣們齊聲高呼。

宴會過後自然是舞會。新郎新娘要一起跳玫瑰之舞，國王答應要吹笛子。他技巧極差，卻從來沒有人敢跟他說實話，因為他是國王。其實他只會兩首旋律，而且老是把兩首搞混，不過無所謂，因為不管他吹奏什麼，大家都會高喊：「吹得好！吹得妙！」

最後一個節目是大型煙火秀，預訂在午夜整點施放。小公主長這麼大從未看過煙火，因此國王下令要御用煙火師出席這場婚禮。

「煙火是什麼樣子？」某天早晨，公主在露台上散步時問王子。

「就像北極光，」國王說道，他總喜歡替人回答問題。「只不過自然得多。比起星星，我個人更喜歡煙火，因為你總會知道它何時出現，而且它就像我吹的笛子一樣令人愉快。你一定得瞧瞧。」

hand in hand under a canopy of purple velvet embroidered with little pearls. Then there was a State Banquet, which lasted for five hours. The Prince and Princess sat at the top of the Great Hall and drank out of a cup of clear crystal. Only true lovers could drink out of this cup, for if false lips touched it, it grew grey and dull and cloudy.

"It's quite clear that they love each other," said the little Page, "as clear as crystal!" and the King doubled his salary a second time. "What an honour!" cried all the courtiers.

After the banquet there was to be a Ball. The bride and bridegroom were to dance the Rose-dance together, and the King had promised to play the flute. He played very badly, but no one had ever dared to tell him so, because he was the King. Indeed, he knew only two airs, and was never quite certain which one he was playing; but it made no matter, for, whatever he did, everybody cried out, "Charming! charming!"

The last item on the programme was a grand display of fireworks, to be let off exactly at midnight. The little Princess had never seen a firework in her life, so the King had given orders that the Royal Pyrotechnist should be in attendance on the day of her marriage.

"What are fireworks like?" she had asked the Prince, one morning, as she was walking on the terrace.

"They are like the Aurora Borealis," said the King, who always answered questions that were addressed to other people, "only much more natural. I prefer them to stars myself, as you always know when they are going to appear, and they are as delightful as my own flute-playing. You must certainly see them."

此時在國王花園的另一頭已搭起高台，御用煙火師將一切準備就緒後，一眾煙火立刻交談起來。

「世界真的美極了，」一支小爆竹大喊道：「光看那些黃色鬱金香就知道了。哇！就算它們是真的煙火炮，也不可能更美了。幸好我到處遊歷過，遊歷能大大提升見識，消除所有的個人偏見。」

「國王的花園又不是全世界，你這支笨爆竹。」一支大型的羅馬蠟燭煙火說：「世界非常巨大，要全部看過一遍得花上三天。」

「只要是你愛的地方就是你的世界。」彷彿心事重重的凱瑟琳轉輪煙火尖聲喊道，早年她曾迷戀過一只舊舊的松木箱，並為自己的心碎感到自豪。「但愛情已不再流行，被詩人給扼殺了。都怪他們寫了太多愛情，結果現在都沒人相信了，我一點也不驚訝。真愛是痛苦的，也是沉默的。我記得我曾經……算了，不說也罷。浪漫已經是過去的事。」

「胡說！」羅馬蠟燭說：「浪漫永遠不會死。它會像月亮一樣，永生不死。譬如說，新郎和新娘就深愛著對方。今天早上我聽一個牛皮紙套筒說了好多，他剛好跟我待在同一個抽屜，宮裡的最新消息他都知道。」

但凱瑟琳轉輪還是搖頭，喃喃自語：「浪漫已死，浪漫已死，浪漫已死。」有人認為同一件事一再反覆說許多次，最後終會成真，她就是其一。

So at the end of the King's garden a great stand had been set up, and as soon as the Royal Pyrotechnist had put everything in its proper place, the fireworks began to talk to each other.

"The world is certainly very beautiful," cried a little Squib. "Just look at those yellow tulips. Why! if they were real crackers they could not be lovelier. I am very glad I have travelled. Travel improves the mind wonderfully, and does away with all one's prejudices."

"The King's garden is not the world, you foolish squib," said a big Roman Candle; "the world is an enormous place, and it would take you three days to see it thoroughly."

"Any place you love is the world to you," exclaimed a pensive Catherine Wheel, who had been attached to an old deal box in early life, and prided herself on her broken heart; "but love is not fashionable any more, the poets have killed it. They wrote so much about it that nobody believed them, and I am not surprised. True love suffers, and is silent. I remember myself once—But it is no matter now. Romance is a thing of the past."

"Nonsense!" said the Roman Candle, "Romance never dies. It is like the moon, and lives for ever. The bride and bridegroom, for instance, love each other very dearly. I heard all about them this morning from a brown-paper cartridge, who happened to be staying in the same drawer as myself, and knew the latest Court news."

But the Catherine Wheel shook her head. "Romance is dead, Romance is dead, Romance is dead," she murmured. She was one of those people who think that, if you say the same thing over and over a great many times, it becomes true in the end.

突然間，響起一聲尖銳的乾咳，大夥兒全都四下張望。

　　出聲的是一支高大的火箭炮，被綁在一根長棍末端，一副不可一世的樣子。他每次發表意見前總要咳個一兩聲，吸引注意力。

　　「嗯哼！嗯哼！」他出聲了，大家都豎耳傾聽，只有可憐的凱瑟琳轉輪還在頻頻搖頭喃喃低語：「浪漫已死。」

　　「肅靜！肅靜！」一枚拉炮喊道。他有幾分政客的味道，在地方選舉中總是極為活躍，對於議會用語知之甚詳。

　　「死絕了。」凱瑟琳轉輪輕聲說完便逕自睡去。

　　等到四下鴉雀無聲，火箭炮又咳了第三聲才開始說話。他的聲音緩慢而清晰，彷彿在口述回憶錄，而且總是隨時留意著交談對象的一舉一動。事實上，他儀表堂堂，無人能及。

　　「國王的兒子何其幸運，」他說道：「能夠在我被施放的當天結婚！說真的，若非事先安排好，他也不可能有這麼好的運氣。但話說回來，王子總是幸運的。」

　　「天哪！」小爆竹說：「我覺得應該恰好相反吧，是我們托王子的福才能被施放。」

　　「你們的情況或許是這樣，」他回答道：「不，我確信你們是這樣沒錯，但我就不同了。我可是非常出色的火

Suddenly, a sharp, dry cough was heard, and they all looked round.

It came from a tall, supercilious-looking Rocket, who was tied to the end of a long stick. He always coughed before he made any observation, so as to attract attention.

"Ahem! ahem!" he said, and everybody listened except the poor Catherine Wheel, who was still shaking her head, and murmuring, "Romance is dead."

"Order! order!" cried out a Cracker. He was something of a politician, and had always taken a prominent part in the local elections, so he knew the proper Parliamentary expressions to use.

"Quite dead," whispered the Catherine Wheel, and she went off to sleep.

As soon as there was perfect silence, the Rocket coughed a third time and began. He spoke with a very slow, distinct voice, as if he was dictating his memoirs, and always looked over the shoulder of the person to whom he was talking. In fact, he had a most distinguished manner.

"How fortunate it is for the King's son," he remarked, "that he is to be married on the very day on which I am to be let off. Really, if it had been arranged beforehand, it could not have turned out better for him; but, Princes are always lucky."

"Dear me!" said the little Squib, "I thought it was quite the other way, and that we were to be let off in the Prince's honour."

"It may be so with you," he answered; "indeed, I have no doubt that it is, but with me it is different. I am a very remarkable Rocket,

箭炮，父母也都很出色。我母親在當年是最知名的凱瑟琳轉輪煙火，以優雅的舞姿著稱。當她在公開場合盛大登場，總會旋轉十九次才熄滅，而且每轉一圈就往空中拋灑七顆粉紅色星星。她直徑長達一米，以最上等的火藥製成。我父親和我一樣是火箭炮，系出法國。他直衝九霄雲外，眾人擔心他會一去不返，但他還是回來了，因為他性情隨和，而且是化做一陣璀璨的金雨落下。報紙極盡吹捧之能事，報導他的表演，就連宮廷公報也說他是『演』火技藝的至高成就。」

「『煙』火技藝，你是說煙火技藝吧，」一枚孟加拉彩光煙火說：「我知道是煙火沒錯，我看見我的罐子上是這麼寫的。」

「我說是『演』火，」火箭炮以嚴厲的語氣回答，孟加拉彩光深受打擊，立刻轉頭去欺負小爆竹，以證明自己還是有點分量。

「我剛剛說，」火箭炮接續道：「我剛剛說……我剛剛說什麼來著？」

「你在說你自己。」羅馬蠟燭回應道。

「可不是嘛，我就知道我剛剛在談論有趣的話題，偏偏被冒冒失失地打斷。各種粗魯無禮的言行，我都深惡痛絕，因為我非常敏感，這世上沒有人像我這麼敏感，這點我相當確定。」

「什麼叫敏感？」拉炮問羅馬蠟燭。

and come of remarkable parents. My mother was the most celebrated Catherine Wheel of her day, and was renowned for her graceful dancing. When she made her great public appearance she spun round nineteen times before she went out, and each time that she did so she threw into the air seven pink stars. She was three feet and a half in diameter, and made of the very best gunpowder. My father was a Rocket like myself, and of French extraction. He flew so high that the people were afraid that he would never come down again. He did, though, for he was of a kindly disposition, and he made a most brilliant descent in a shower of golden rain. The newspapers wrote about his performance in very flattering terms. Indeed, the Court Gazette called him a triumph of Pylotechnic art."

"Pyrotechnic, Pyrotechnic, you mean," said a Bengal Light; "I know it is Pyrotechnic, for I saw it written on my own canister."

"Well, I said Pylotechnic," answered the Rocket, in a severe tone of voice, and the Bengal Light felt so crushed that he began at once to bully the little squibs, in order to show that he was still a person of some importance.

"I was saying," continued the Rocket, "I was saying—What was I saying?"

"You were talking about yourself," replied the Roman Candle.

"Of course; I knew I was discussing some interesting subject when I was so rudely interrupted. I hate rudeness and bad manners of every kind, for I am extremely sensitive. No one in the whole world is so sensitive as I am, I am quite sure of that."

"What is a sensitive person?" said the Cracker to the Roman

「就是說自己長雞眼，就老是去踩別人的腳。」羅馬蠟燭低聲回答，拉炮聽了差點笑破肚皮。

「請問你在笑什麼？」火箭炮正經地問道：「我又沒笑。」

「我笑是因為我高興。」拉炮回答。

「這個理由太自私了。」火箭炮氣憤地說：「你有什麼權利高興？你應該為別人想想。事實上，你應該為我想想。我隨時都想著我自己，也期望其他人都能想著我，這就叫同情心。這是一種美德，我便高度具有這種美德。舉例來說，萬一今晚我出了任何差錯，對所有人是多大的不幸！王子和公主再也無法幸福，他們的婚姻生活全都毀了，至於國王，我知道他將永遠無法平復心情。說實話，每當我反思自己的重要地位，幾乎都會感動到掉淚。」

「你要是想為眾人帶來歡樂，最好別把自己弄濕了。」羅馬蠟燭高喊。

「那可不，這只是一般常識。」孟加拉彩光高呼，他現在心情好些了。

「一般常識，說得對啊！」火箭炮憤慨地說：「你們忘了嗎？我是非常不一般、非常出色的。哼，凡是沒有想像力的人，都可能擁有常識。可是我有想像力，我思考事情從不依實際情況，而總是用截然不同的角度看事情。至

Candle.

"A person who, because he has corns himself, always treads on other people's toes," answered the Roman Candle in a low whisper; and the Cracker nearly exploded with laughter.

"Pray, what are you laughing at?" inquired the Rocket; "I am not laughing."

"I am laughing because I am happy," replied the Cracker.

"That is a very selfish reason," said the Rocket angrily. "What right have you to be happy? You should be thinking about others. In fact, you should be thinking about me. I am always thinking about myself, and I expect everybody else to do the same. That is what is called sympathy. It is a beautiful virtue, and I possess it in a high degree. Suppose, for instance, anything happened to me to-night, what a misfortune that would be for every one! The Prince and Princess would never be happy again, their whole married life would be spoiled; and as for the King, I know he would not get over it. Really, when I begin to reflect on the importance of my position, I am almost moved to tears."

"If you want to give pleasure to others," cried the Roman Candle, "you had better keep yourself dry."

"Certainly," exclaimed the Bengal Light, who was now in better spirits; "that is only common sense."

"Common sense, indeed!" said the Rocket indignantly; "you forget that I am very uncommon, and very remarkable. Why, anybody can have common sense, provided that they have no imagination. But I have imagination, for I never think of things as they really are; I

於說別把自己弄濕，看來這裡的各位都不懂得欣賞感情豐富的天性。幸好我並不在乎。能夠支撐一個人度過一生的唯一動力，就是要意識到其他人都差自己一大截，而這正是我一直以來培養的感覺。可是你們一個個都鐵石心腸，竟然在這裡嬉笑玩鬧，好像王子公主不是剛剛新婚似的。」

「拜託，為什麼不可以？」一顆小煙火氣球尖叫：「這可是天大的喜事，等我飛上天，我打算把全部的事都講給星星們聽。當我說起美麗的新娘，你會看見它們一閃一閃地猛眨眼睛。」

「哈！多卑微的觀念啊！」火箭炮說：「但這完全在我意料之中。你什麼都不懂，腦袋裡空空如也。我說呀，也許王子公主會去住在河川流過的鄉間，也許他們只會生一個兒子，一個金髮的小男孩，眼睛和王子一樣是紫羅蘭色；也許有一天他會和保母出外散步；也許保母會在接骨木下睡著；也許小男孩會跌落深深的河水中淹死。這是多麼不幸的遭遇！可憐哪，失去了唯一的兒子！真是太令人悲痛了！換作是我，這個傷痛永遠也無法平復。」

「但他們又還沒有失去獨生子。」羅馬蠟燭說：「他們根本還沒遭遇任何不幸。」

「我也沒說他們遭遇了不幸。」火箭炮回答：「我是說也許。假如他們已經失去獨生子，那麼多說也無益。我

always think of them as being quite different. As for keeping myself dry, there is evidently no one here who can at all appreciate an emotional nature. Fortunately for myself, I don't care. The only thing that sustains one through life is the consciousness of the immense inferiority of everybody else, and this is a feeling that I have always cultivated. But none of you have any hearts. Here you are laughing and making merry just as if the Prince and Princess had not just been married."

"Well, really," exclaimed a small Fire-balloon, "why not? It is a most joyful occasion, and when I soar up into the air I intend to tell the stars all about it. You will see them twinkle when I talk to them about the pretty bride."

"Ah! what a trivial view of life!" said the Rocket; "but it is only what I expected. There is nothing in you; you are hollow and empty. Why, perhaps the Prince and Princess may go to live in a country where there is a deep river, and perhaps they may have one only son, a little fair-haired boy with violet eyes like the Prince himself; and perhaps some day he may go out to walk with his nurse; and perhaps the nurse may go to sleep under a great elder-tree; and perhaps the little boy may fall into the deep river and be drowned. What a terrible misfortune! Poor people, to lose their only son! It is really too dreadful! I shall never get over it."

"But they have not lost their only son," said the Roman Candle; "no misfortune has happened to them at all."

"I never said that they had," replied the Rocket; "I said that they might. If they had lost their only son there would be no use in saying

最討厭那些事後懊悔的人。但是一想到他們可能會失去獨生子，我就難過到不能自己。」

「那是當然了！」孟加拉彩光嚷嚷道：「說句實話，你是我見過最裝模作樣到不能自己的傢伙。」

「你才是我所見過最粗魯的人，」火箭炮說：「你不可能明白我對王子的情誼。」

「拜託，你根本不認識他。」羅馬蠟燭咆哮。

「我又沒說我認識他，」火箭炮說：「我敢說我要是認識他，應該根本不會和他當朋友。認識自己的朋友是件危險的事。」

「我說真的，你最好還是別把自己弄濕，這才是要緊事。」煙火氣球說。

「對你來說很重要，這我絕對相信，但我想哭就哭。」火箭炮說完果真哭了起來，淚水如雨滴般滑下棍子，險些淹死兩隻小甲蟲；這兩隻甲蟲打算成家，正在尋找一個乾燥舒適的居住地。

「他想必的確天生浪漫，沒什麼好哭也能哭得出來。」凱瑟琳轉輪說著便深深嘆了口氣，她又想起了那只松木箱子。

但是羅馬蠟燭和孟加拉彩光憤怒不已，不停扯開嗓子喊著：「耍花招！耍花招！」他們倆都極度務實，只要看什麼不順眼，就說是耍花招。

這時月亮升起，宛如一面神奇的銀盾，群星也開始閃

anything more about the matter. I hate people who cry over spilt milk. But when I think that they might lose their only son, I certainly am very much affected."

"You certainly are!" cried the Bengal Light. "In fact, you are the most affected person I ever met."

"You are the rudest person I ever met," said the Rocket, "and you cannot understand my friendship for the Prince."

"Why, you don't even know him," growled the Roman Candle.

"I never said I knew him," answered the Rocket. "I dare say that if I knew him I should not be his friend at all. It is a very dangerous thing to know one's friends."

"You had really better keep yourself dry," said the Fire-balloon. "That is the important thing."

"Very important for you, I have no doubt," answered the Rocket, "but I shall weep if I choose"; and he actually burst into real tears, which flowed down his stick like rain-drops, and nearly drowned two little beetles, who were just thinking of setting up house together, and were looking for a nice dry spot to live in.

"He must have a truly romantic nature," said the Catherine Wheel, "for he weeps when there is nothing at all to weep about"; and she heaved a deep sigh, and thought about the deal box.

But the Roman Candle and the Bengal Light were quite indignant, and kept saying, "Humbug! humbug!" at the top of their voices. They were extremely practical, and whenever they objected to anything they called it humbug.

Then the moon rose like a wonderful silver shield; and the stars

閃發光，宮殿裡傳來了音樂聲。

王子公主為眾人開舞。二人舞姿曼妙，窗邊高大的白色百合忍不住往內偷看，碩大的紅罌粟也跟著點頭打拍子。

接著十點的鐘聲響起，而後十一點，而後十二點，就在午夜最後一聲鐘響，所有人都來到露台上，國王也命人去請來御用煙火師。

開始放煙火吧，國王說道。御用煙火師深深一鞠躬，便大步走向花園另一頭。他帶了六名助手，每人各持一柄火把。

表演場面確實壯觀。

咻！咻！凱瑟琳轉輪轉啊轉，轉個不停。轟！轟！羅馬蠟燭發射。接著是小爆竹滿場飛舞，孟加拉彩光照得四周紅通通。「再見了！」煙火氣球大喊，同時高飛遠去，藍色小火星紛落。砰！砰！拉炮興高采烈地回應著。大夥都非常成功，只有了不起的火箭炮因為哭得渾身濕透，根本無法發射。他最值得稱道的就是火藥，卻因為被淚水浸濕而無用武之地。他平時不屑與那些窮酸親戚交談，頂多只是對他們冷笑一聲，此時親戚們卻個個竄升天際，宛如綺麗的金花綻放出火紅的花瓣。「好哇！好哇！」宮廷眾人歡呼道，小公主也笑得開懷。

「我猜他們是要把我留到某個重要場合，一定是這樣

began to shine, and a sound of music came from the palace.

The Prince and Princess were leading the dance. They danced so beautifully that the tall white lilies peeped in at the window and watched them, and the great red poppies nodded their heads and beat time.

Then ten o'clock struck, and then eleven, and then twelve, and at the last stroke of midnight every one came out on the terrace, and the King sent for the Royal Pyrotechnist.

"Let the fireworks begin," said the King; and the Royal Pyrotechnist made a low bow, and marched down to the end of the garden. He had six attendants with him, each of whom carried a lighted torch at the end of a long pole.

It was certainly a magnificent display.

Whizz! Whizz! went the Catherine Wheel, as she spun round and round. Boom! Boom! went the Roman Candle. Then the Squibs danced all over the place, and the Bengal Lights made everything look scarlet. "Good-bye," cried the Fire-balloon, as he soared away, dropping tiny blue sparks. Bang! Bang! answered the Crackers, who were enjoying themselves immensely. Every one was a great success except the Remarkable Rocket. He was so damp with crying that he could not go off at all. The best thing in him was the gunpowder, and that was so wet with tears that it was of no use. All his poor relations, to whom he would never speak, except with a sneer, shot up into the sky like wonderful golden flowers with blossoms of fire. Huzza! Huzza! cried the Court; and the little Princess laughed with pleasure.

"I suppose they are reserving me for some grand occasion," said

沒錯。」火箭炮說，神態更加地不可一世。

　　第二天，工人前來整理現場。「他們顯然是代表團，」火箭炮說：「我得展現應有的尊嚴來迎接他們。」於是他鼻孔朝天，煞有介事地皺起眉頭，彷彿在思考非常重要的議題。但工人根本沒注意到他，直到臨走前，才有一人無意中瞥見他。「唉呀！」他大喊一聲：「這麼粗製濫造的火箭炮！」說著隨手便將火箭炮丟出牆外，掉入了水溝。

　　「**粗製濫造？粗製濫造？**」火箭炮在空中飛旋時喃喃說道：「不可能！那個人說的是『**高貴華麗**』。**粗製濫造**和**高貴華麗**聽起來差不多，事實上往往是一樣的意思。」他隨後跌入泥巴裡。

　　「這裡不舒服，」他說道：「但這無疑是某種時下流行的水療浴場，他們送我來是為了讓我恢復健康。我的神經確實消耗得很嚴重，需要休息一下。」

　　這時，有一隻小青蛙朝他游來，他一雙眼睛亮得像是鑲了寶石，身上穿著一件斑斑點點的綠色外衣。

　　「啊，有個新來的！」青蛙說：「對嘛，畢竟什麼都比不上泥巴。我只要有雨天和水溝，就很快樂了。你覺得今天下午會下雨嗎？我真希望會，偏偏天空那麼藍，又沒有雲，太可惜了！」

　　「嗯哼！嗯哼！」火箭炮出聲後開始咳嗽。

　　「你的聲音真討人喜歡！」青蛙高喊：「還真像青蛙

the Rocket; "no doubt that is what it means," and he looked more supercilious than ever.

The next day the workmen came to put everything tidy. "This is evidently a deputation," said the Rocket; "I will receive them with becoming dignity" so he put his nose in the air, and began to frown severely as if he were thinking about some very important subject. But they took no notice of him at all till they were just going away. Then one of them caught sight of him. "Hallo!" he cried, "what a bad rocket!" and he threw him over the wall into the ditch.

"Bad Rocket? Bad Rocket?" he said, as he whirled through the air; "impossible! Grand Rocket, that is what the man said. Bad and Grand sound very much the same, indeed they often are the same"; and he fell into the mud.

"It is not comfortable here," he remarked, "but no doubt it is some fashionable watering-place, and they have sent me away to recruit my health. My nerves are certainly very much shattered, and I require rest."

Then a little Frog, with bright jewelled eyes, and a green mottled coat, swam up to him.

"A new arrival, I see!" said the Frog. "Well, after all there is nothing like mud. Give me rainy weather and a ditch, and I am quite happy. Do you think it will be a wet afternoon? I am sure I hope so, but the sky is quite blue and cloudless. What a pity!"

"Ahem! ahem!" said the Rocket, and he began to cough.

"What a delightful voice you have!" cried the Frog. "Really it is quite like a croak, and croaking is of course the most musical sound in

嘓嘓叫，而青蛙的叫聲當然是世界上最美妙的聲音了。今晚你就會聽見我們大合唱。我們會坐在農舍旁的舊養鴨池裡，等月亮一升起，就開始合唱。因為我們的歌聲太令人著迷，人人都清醒著，躺在床上聆聽。不瞞你說，昨天我才聽見農夫的老婆對她母親說，我們讓她一整夜都沒能闔眼。看見自己這麼受歡迎，實在太痛快了。」

「嗯哼！嗯哼！」火箭炮生氣地說。他一句話也插不上，著惱不已。

「的確是討人喜歡的聲音。」青蛙又接著說：「希望你能到養鴨池來合唱。我要去找我女兒了。我有六個漂亮的女兒，我很擔心她們碰上狗魚。那傢伙完全就是個禽獸，會毫不猶豫吃掉她們當早餐。好吧，再見了，和你聊天真的很開心。」

「還聊天呢！」火箭炮說：「從頭到尾都是你一個人在說，這哪叫聊天？」

「總得有人聽啊，」青蛙回答：「而且我喜歡全部由我一個人說，這樣省時間又能避免爭吵。」

「但我就是喜歡爭吵。」火箭炮說。

「不會吧，」青蛙自以為是地說：「爭吵是最粗俗的了，在理想的社會裡，每個人的意見都會完全一致。再次說聲再見，我已經遠遠地看到我女兒。」小青蛙隨即游開。

「真是惹人生氣，」火箭炮說：「也太沒教養。我最

the world. You will hear our glee-club this evening. We sit in the old duck pond close by the farmer's house, and as soon as the moon rises we begin. It is so entrancing that everybody lies awake to listen to us. In fact, it was only yesterday that I heard the farmer's wife say to her mother that she could not get a wink of sleep at night on account of us. It is most gratifying to find oneself so popular."

"Ahem! ahem!" said the Rocket angrily. He was very much annoyed that he could not get a word in.

"A delightful voice, certainly," continued the Frog; "I hope you will come over to the duck-pond. I am off to look for my daughters. I have six beautiful daughters, and I am so afraid the Pike may meet them. He is a perfect monster, and would have no hesitation in breakfasting off them. Well, good-bye: I have enjoyed our conversation very much, I assure you."

"Conversation, indeed!" said the Rocket. "You have talked the whole time yourself. That is not conversation."

"Somebody must listen," answered the Frog, "and I like to do all the talking myself. It saves time, and prevents arguments."

"But I like arguments," said the Rocket.

"I hope not," said the Frog complacently. "Arguments are extremely vulgar, for everybody in good society holds exactly the same opinions. Good-bye a second time; I see my daughters in the distance;" and the little Frog swam away.

"You are a very irritating person," said the Rocket, "and very ill-bred. I hate people who talk about themselves, as you do, when one wants to talk about oneself, as I do. It is what I call selfishness, and

討厭這種人了，有人想說說自己的事，比方像我，偏偏有人一直在說他們自己的事，就像你。這正是我說的自私，自私是最可恨的，尤其對我這種以天生富有同情心而聞名的人來說更是如此。老實說，你應該拿我做榜樣，天底下找不到比我更好的模範了。你應該趁現在好好把握機會，因為我差不多馬上就要回宮了。說實話，我在宮裡非常受寵，昨天王子和公主還為了向我表達敬意而結婚。當然了，這些事你一無所知，因為你是個鄉巴佬。」

「跟他說也沒用了，」一隻歇在寬大褐色香蒲葉的蜻蜓說道：「一點用都沒有，因為他已經走了。」

「那是他的損失，不是我的。」火箭炮回答：「我才不會只因為他不理睬，就不再跟他說話。我喜歡聽自己說話，這是我最大的樂趣之一。我經常自言自語老半天，我實在太聰明了，有時候連我自己也是一個字都聽不懂。」

「那你真該去講授哲學課。」蜻蜓說著展開美麗的薄紗翅膀，飛上天去。

「他竟然不待下來，實在太傻了！」火箭炮說：「這種提升心靈的機會肯定不常有。不過，我才不在乎。我的才情總有一天一定會受到賞識。」他往泥中陷得更深了些。

過了一會兒，有隻大白鴨游了過來。她有一雙黃色的腳，腳上帶蹼，由於走路搖曳生姿，是公認的大美人。

selfishness is a most detestable thing, especially to any one of my temperament, for I am well known for my sympathetic nature. In fact, you should take example by me; you could not possibly have a better model. Now that you have the chance you had better avail yourself of it, for I am going back to Court almost immediately. I am a great favourite at Court; in fact, the Prince and Princess were married yesterday in my honour. Of course you know nothing of these matters, for you are a provincial."

"There is no good talking to him," said a Dragon-fly, who was sitting on the top of a large brown bulrush; "no good at all, for he has gone away."

"Well, that is his loss, not mine," answered the Rocket. "I am not going to stop talking to him merely because he pays no attention. I like hearing myself talk. It is one of my greatest pleasures. I often have long conversations all by myself, and I am so clever that sometimes I don't understand a single word of what I am saying."

"Then you should certainly lecture on Philosophy," said the Dragon-fly; and he spread a pair of lovely gauze wings and soared away into the sky.

"How very silly of him not to stay here!" said the Rocket. "I am sure that he has not often got such a chance of improving his mind. However, I don't care a bit. Genius like mine is sure to be appreciated some day"; and he sank down a little deeper into the mud.

After some time a large White Duck swam up to him. She had yellow legs, and webbed feet, and was considered a great beauty on account of her waddle.

「呱呱呱，」她說：「你的模樣真奇怪！能不能請問你是天生長這樣，還是出過意外？」

「看得出來你一直住在鄉下，」火箭炮回答：「否則就會知道我是誰。不過我原諒你的無知，我總不能奢望別人都和自己一樣出色。妳要是聽說我能飛上天空，變成一陣金雨落下，肯定會很驚訝。」

「我覺得這沒什麼，」鴨子說：「我看不出這對任何人能有什麼好處。唔，如果你能像牛一樣耕田，像馬一樣拉車，像牧羊犬一樣看顧羊群，那才叫了不起。」

「這位鴨女士，」火箭炮以非常高傲的語氣大聲說：「看來你是屬於低下階層。我這種身分的人從來就沒有用處，我們達到一些成就也就綽綽有餘了。我本身並不贊成任何形式的勤奮，而你似乎頗為稱道的那些形式，這就更不用說了。說實話，我始終認為辛苦工作只是那些無所事事的人逃避的方式。」

「好啦，好啦，」鴨子說道，她個性十分平和，從不與人爭執。「各有所好嘛。無論如何，希望你在這裡定居下來。」

「噢，當然不了！」火箭炮大喊：「我只是個訪客，一個尊貴的訪客。其實我覺得這裡很無聊，既沒有社交活動，也不能安靜獨處。老實說，基本上就是郊外。我很可

"Quack, quack, quack," she said. "What a curious shape you are! May I ask were you born like that, or is it the result of an accident?"

"It is quite evident that you have always lived in the country," answered the Rocket, "otherwise you would know who I am. However, I excuse your ignorance. It would be unfair to expect other people to be as remarkable as oneself. You will no doubt be surprised to hear that I can fly up into the sky, and come down in a shower of golden rain."

"I don't think much of that," said the Duck, "as I cannot see what use it is to any one. Now, if you could plough the fields like the ox, or draw a cart like the horse, or look after the sheep like the collie-dog, that would be something."

"My good creature," cried the Rocket in a very haughty tone of voice, "I see that you belong to the lower orders. A person of my position is never useful. We have certain accomplishments, and that is more than sufficient. I have no sympathy myself with industry of any kind, least of all with such industries as you seem to recommend. Indeed, I have always been of opinion that hard work is simply the refuge of people who have nothing whatever to do."

"Well, well," said the Duck, who was of a very peaceable disposition, and never quarrelled with any one, "everybody has different tastes. I hope, at any rate, that you are going to take up your residence here."

"Oh! dear no," cried the Rocket. "I am merely a visitor, a distinguished visitor. The fact is that I find this place rather tedious. There is neither society here, nor solitude. In fact, it is essentially

能還是會回到宮裡，因為我知道自己注定要轟動全世界。」

　　「我自己也曾一度想要參與公眾事務，」鴨子說：「有太多事需要改革了。事實上，不久前我還當過一場會議的主席，會上通過決議，要譴責一切我們不喜歡的事。然而，成效似乎不大。現在我已回歸家庭生活，照顧家人。」

　　「我是天生的公眾人物，」火箭炮說：「我所有的親戚都是，即使最卑微的幾位也不例外。每當我們上場，就會大受關注。我自己還沒有真正上場過，但只要我一登場，場面必定非比尋常。家庭生活會讓人老得快，而忽略更崇高的事。」

　　「呵，人生更崇高的事，多美好呀！」鴨子說：「我這才想起我有多餓。」她於是順流游開，一面叫著：「呱呱呱。」

　　「回來！回來呀！」火箭炮叫嚷著：「我有好多話要跟你說。」但鴨子不理他，他便自言自語道：「走了也好，她根本是中產階級的心性。」他又往泥巴裡陷得更深一些，開始思及天才的孤獨。這時忽然出現兩個穿著白罩衫的小男孩，帶著一只水壺和一些柴火跑下堤坡。

　　「他們一定是來迎接我的代表團。」火箭炮說著極力擺出莊嚴高貴的樣子。

suburban. I shall probably go back to Court, for I know that I am destined to make a sensation in the world."

"I had thoughts of entering public life once myself," remarked the Duck; "there are so many things that need reforming. Indeed, I took the chair at a meeting some time ago, and we passed resolutions condemning everything that we did not like. However, they did not seem to have much effect. Now I go in for domesticity, and look after my family."

"I am made for public life," said the Rocket, "and so are all my relations, even the humblest of them. Whenever we appear we excite great attention. I have not actually appeared myself, but when I do so it will be a magnificent sight. As for domesticity, it ages one rapidly, and distracts one's mind from higher things."

"Ah! the higher things of life, how fine they are!" said the Duck; "and that reminds me how hungry I feel": and she swam away down the stream, saying, "Quack, quack, quack."

"Come back! come back!" screamed the Rocket, "I have a great deal to say to you"; but the Duck paid no attention to him. "I am glad that she has gone," he said to himself, "she has a decidedly middle-class mind"; and he sank a little deeper still into the mud, and began to think about the loneliness of genius, when suddenly two little boys in white smocks came running down the bank, with a kettle and some faggots.

"This must be the deputation," said the Rocket, and he tried to look very dignified.

「哇！」其中一個男孩喊道：「你看這根舊棍子，不知道是從哪來的。」他隨手拾起溝裡的火箭炮。

「舊棍子！」火箭炮說：「不可能！他說的是『金棍子』。說金棍子未免太抬舉我了，他看來把我誤認為宮中顯貴了呢。」

「我們把它丟進火裡吧！」另一個男孩說：「可以拿來燒水。」

於是他們堆起柴火，將火箭炮放在最上面，點了火。

「太棒了，」火箭炮高喊：「他們要在大白天施放我，好讓所有人都能看見。」

「我們先睡一覺，等睡醒的時候水也燒開了。」他們說完便躺在草地上，闔上眼睛。

火箭炮全身濕漉漉，花了很長時間才點燃。不過終於還是成功燒起來了。

「我現在要發射了！」他放聲大喊，身子挺得筆直。「我知道我會飛得遠比星星還高，遠比月亮還高，遠比太陽還高。說實話，我會飛到高過……」

嘶！嘶！嘶！他一飛沖天。

「好耶！」他高喊：「我要像這樣飛一輩子。我是多麼成功啊！」

可是沒有人看見。

接著他開始覺得渾身有種奇怪的刺痛感。

「我現在要爆開了，」他大喊：「我要引爆全世界，

"Hallo!" cried one of the boys, "look at this old stick! I wonder how it came here"; and he picked the rocket out of the ditch.

"Old Stick!" said the Rocket, "impossible! Gold Stick, that is what he said. Gold Stick is very complimentary. In fact, he mistakes me for one of the Court dignitaries!"

"Let us put it into the fire!" said the other boy, "it will help to boil the kettle."

So they piled the faggots together, and put the Rocket on top, and lit the fire.

"This is magnificent," cried the Rocket, "they are going to let me off in broad day-light, so that every one can see me."

"We will go to sleep now," they said, "and when we wake up the kettle will be boiled"; and they lay down on the grass, and shut their eyes.

The Rocket was very damp, so he took a long time to burn. At last, however, the fire caught him.

"Now I am going off!" he cried, and he made himself very stiff and straight. "I know I shall go much higher than the stars, much higher than the moon, much higher than the sun. In fact, I shall go so high that—"

Fizz! Fizz! Fizz! and he went straight up into the air.

"Delightful!" he cried, "I shall go on like this for ever. What a success I am!"

But nobody saw him.

Then he began to feel a curious tingling sensation all over him.

"Now I am going to explode," he cried. "I shall set the whole

要鬧得震天響，讓接下來一整年誰都不會談論其他事情。」他的確爆開了。砰！砰！砰！火藥爆發。毫無疑問。

可是沒有人聽見，連那兩個小男孩也聽不見，因為他們睡得正香。

這時候他全身上下只剩棍子，掉下來正好落在一隻在溝邊散步的鵝背上。

「我的天哪！」鵝大叫一聲：「要下棍子雨了。」說完連忙下水去。

「我就知道我會引起大轟動。」火箭炮喘著氣說，然後就熄滅了。

 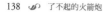

world on fire, and make such a noise that nobody will talk about anything else for a whole year." And he certainly did explode. Bang! Bang! Bang! went the gunpowder. There was no doubt about it.

But nobody heard him, not even the two little boys, for they were sound asleep.

Then all that was left of him was the stick, and this fell down on the back of a Goose who was taking a walk by the side of the ditch.

"Good heavens!" cried the Goose. "It is going to rain sticks"; and she rushed into the water.

"I knew I should create a great sensation," gasped the Rocket, and he went out.

Golden Age 47

快樂王子【復刻1888年初版插畫】
王爾德世紀末唯美主義童話代表作｜中英雙語（唯美精裝版）
The Happy Prince and Other Tales

作　　者	奧斯卡‧王爾德 Oscar Wilde
譯　　者	顏湘如

野人文化股份有限公司

社　　長	張瑩瑩
總 編 輯	蔡麗真
副 主 編	徐子涵
責任編輯	陳瑞瑤
專業校對	魏秋綢
行銷經理	林麗紅
行銷企畫	蔡逸萱、李映柔
封面設計	莊謹銘
美術設計	洪素貞

讀書共和國出版集團

社　　長	郭重興
發 行 人	曾大福
業務平臺總經理	李雪麗
業務平臺副總經理	李復民
實體通路組	林詩富、陳志峰、郭文弘、王文賓、賴佩瑜、周宥騰
網路暨海外通路組	張鑫峰、林裴瑤、范光杰
特版通路組	陳綺瑩、郭文龍
電子商務組	黃詩芸、林雅卿、高崇哲、沈宗俊
專案企劃組	蔡孟庭、盤惟心
閱讀社群組	黃志堅、羅文浩、盧煒婷
版 權 部	黃知涵
印 務 部	江域平、黃禮賢、李孟儒

出　　版	野人文化股份有限公司
發　　行	遠足文化事業股份有限公司
	地址：231新北市新店區民權路108-2號9樓
	電話：（02）2218-1417　傳真：（02）8667-1065
	電子信箱：service@bookrep.com.tw
	網址：www.bookrep.com.tw
	郵撥帳號：19504465 遠足文化事業股份有限公司
	客服專線：0800-221-029
法律顧問	華洋法律事務所　蘇文生律師
印　　製	呈靖彩印股份有限公司
初版首刷	2022年12月

國家圖書館出版品預行編目（CIP）資料

快樂王子：王爾德世紀末唯美主義童話
代表作／奧斯卡‧王爾德（Oscar Wilde）
作；顏湘如譯 .-- 初版 .-- 新北市：野人
文化股份有限公司出版：遠足文化事業
股份有限公司發行，2022.12
　面；　公分
中英對照
譯自：The Happy Prince and Other Tales

873.596　　　　　　　　　　111016058

ISBN：978-986-384-795-3（精裝）
ISBN：978-986-384-799-1（PDF）
ISBN：978-986-384-800-4（EPUB）

快樂王子

野人文化　　野人文化
官方網頁　　讀者回函

線上讀者回函專用
QR CODE，你的寶
貴意見，將是我們
進步的最大動力。

延伸閱讀

墨利斯的情人 *Maurice*
【20世紀最甜美不朽的同性小說｜同名電影經典原著】
E. M. 佛斯特／著

> 20世紀最勇敢而偉大的愛戀
> E.M. 佛斯特不朽之作

「幸福結局是絕對必要的，
否則我就不必費心去寫它了。」

這是一本勇氣之書，
宛如黑暗中照亮前行的溫柔燈塔，
鼓勵我們勇敢捍衛幸福的權利。

裝幀師 *The Binding*
布莉琪・柯林斯／著

> 英國 Waterstone 書店 2019 年度好書決選／ 2020 年 1 月選書
> 《星期日泰晤士報》Best Seller No.1

年度最浪漫奇幻小說
風靡全英國的禁忌之書
不一樣的反烏托邦愛情故事

如果這世上有一本書，能夠──
抹去你的悲傷。使你忘卻痛苦。為你永遠隱藏一個祕密。
你是否願意不問代價，縱身一試？